GRAVEYARD
SHIFT

ALSO BY M. L. RIO

If We Were Villains

GRAVE YARD SHIFT

A Novella

M. L. Rio

FLATIRON
BOOKS
NEW YORK

GRAVEYARD SHIFT. Copyright © 2024 by Melanie Rio. All rights reserved. Printed in the United States of America. For information, address Flatiron Books, 120 Broadway, New York, NY 10271.

www.flatironbooks.com

Designed by Jen Edwards

Mushroom illustrations © Potapov Alexander / Shutterstock

Library of Congress Cataloging-in-Publication Data

Names: Rio, M. L., author.
Title: Graveyard shift : a novella / M.L. Rio.
Description: First edition. | New York : Flatiron Books, 2024.
Identifiers: LCCN 2024016177 | ISBN 9781250356796
    (trade paperback) | ISBN 9781250356772 (hardcover run-on) |
    ISBN 9781250356789 (ebook)
Subjects: LCGFT: Thrillers (Fiction) | Novellas.
Classification: LCC PS3618.I564 G73 2024 | DDC 813/.6—
    dc23/eng/20240419
LC record available at https://lccn.loc.gov/2024016177

Our books may be purchased in bulk for promotional,
educational, or business use. Please contact your local bookseller
or the Macmillan Corporate and Premium Sales Department
at 1-800-221-7945, extension 5442, or by email at
MacmillanSpecialMarkets@macmillan.com.

First Edition: 2024

10 9 8 7 6 5 4 3 2 1

For my own midnight group text:
Alley Cat, Marge, Paigey, and Hex

Author's Note

Insomnia has been my constant companion since childhood. I had night terrors as a toddler, spent most nights in elementary school reading in my closet past my bedtime, was writing novels by lamplight by middle school, and lived a largely nocturnal existence for most of my twelve years in higher education. You could call me an authority on the nightside of life, where the borders between the real and the illusory dissolve. *Graveyard Shift* lived in my head a long time before my publisher approached me about a novella. I liked the idea of a story about sleep and sleeplessness that could unfold over only one evening, like a shady, troubled dream. It's frighteningly easy to get lost in your own subconscious; any place you think you know is different after dark.

I've always been preoccupied with the intersections of

art and science, and especially the effects of sleep deprivation on cognitive (mal)function. Tellingly, the most arrest-
ing odes to slumber are spoken by those who can't have it.
Consider Macbeth, doomed to sleep no more: slumber is the
"balm of hurt minds," "sore labor's bath," a doting seamstress
who "knits up the ravell'd sleeve of care." Insomnia unrav-
els a person without mercy. The mystery at the heart of
Graveyard Shift is as much about what keeps us up at night
as it is about what's buried in the cemetery. Of course, I
have also been a lurker in churchyards; the proximity of
somebody's final resting place can be a strange comfort when
you can't find any rest of your own. When I was in college,
the tiny plot of plots behind my dormitory was a favorite
place I rarely had to share. But I did occasionally encounter
other insomniacs there, running down the long, dark hours
until morning.

So *Graveyard Shift* took shape, borrowing from a number
of literary traditions as well as my own life experience. My
academic research sits squarely in the medical humanities;
small wonder that this has infiltrated my creative writing.
The necessary disclaimer is that while I am a species of re-
searcher, like Tamar I am not a scientist, and so must beg
forgiveness for any errors in the following pages. Fiction
is, after all, not a clinical trial. But this is not to say its
findings are not statistically significant. During my PhD,
I taught a science fiction course to college students, and
saw firsthand how *Cat's Cradle*, *Where Late the Sweet Birds
Sang*, and even *Jurassic Park* encouraged them to consider

the potential ramifications of new technologies for humans and the planet we inhabit—not just profit margins. Writing a novel is never so purely didactic, but I hope the following pages provide not just a good story to suit the dead hours between midnight and morning but also an invitation to ask probing questions and get your hands dirty digging down under the surface of things.

Sweet dreams.

GRAVEYARD
SHIFT

12:00 AM
Edie

They met in the cemetery every night at midnight. Not on purpose, exactly, but not quite by accident either. University policy prohibited smoking within a hundred feet of any campus building, and on the west side of campus, where the borders between the medical school and the broader community were especially porous, the only place a person gasping for a cigarette could safely stand was in the unkempt graveyard behind the Church of Saint Anthony the Anchorite.

Most of the names on most of the gravestones had been scrubbed out by time or teenage vandals; the church itself had been boarded up and was so overgrown with vines and moss and mold that the DANGER, KEEP OUT sign nailed across the doors was decidedly redundant. Since its designation as a local historic landmark, it was protected from the bulldozers and wrecking balls that had razed everything else south of Azalea Street to make way for more patients, more parking, more gift shops and dining halls. While the medical school constructed, Saint Anthony the Anchorite deconstructed—one brick, one beam at a time. Nobody in their right mind would loiter in its long shadow in the middle of the night, but nobody in their right mind still smoked these days anyway.

So Edie Wu told herself as she trudged across campus from the offices of the *Belltower Times*. She was always the last to clock out—her grim duty as editor-in-chief to lash herself to the masthead, go down with the ship—but lately she didn't clock out so much as take five. Take a break. Take a walk. Tell herself one cigarette a night was not a habit, just a way to take the edge off when she was, well, *on edge*. And when was she not? Yes, it was a student paper, but a six-time Pacemaker Award–winning student paper circulating to ten thousand readers. Her predecessor had graduated and gone on to the *Nation* but still cast a long shadow across Edie's desk. Some nights she wished for catastrophe to strike just so she'd have a big story to break, which only made her feel worse in the morning, because she still had no story, but she did have a fresh black bruise on her conscience.

The bigger problem was The Lump. Since its first appearance two weeks ago, everything had felt hugely, horribly urgent. She pulled her coat a little closer and hurried toward the ramshackle shadow of the Anchorite, a rock-bound black mass rudely eclipsing the sickly sickle moon.

She was huffing and puffing by the time she crested the hill and slipped through the gate, which refused to stay latched anymore. Like the KEEP OUT sign, the gate was redundant. Nobody *wanted* to huddle in a moldering churchyard after midnight because there was nowhere else to smoke. But huddle they did. Misery loved company and made strange bedfellows.

Two of the others had beaten her there. She knew them by their shadows: Tuck, with his hands in his pockets and his shoulders hunched, was always first. Beside him stood Hannah, who put her hood up at the first rustle of autumn and didn't take it down again until May. Oddly, though, they weren't talking. They stared down at the ground in stony imitation of the graveyard angels, without the blank unblinking eyes or patchy beards of lichen. When they heard Edie's footsteps round the Drewalt obelisk, they looked up and she looked down and realized that what they were actually staring at was a hole in the ground.

Edie stared, too. "The fuck is that?"

Hannah took a long drag. "The fuck do you think?" The hood cast her narrow face in shadow, blacked out both her eyes. Of the other Anchorites, Edie liked her least. She turned to Tuck instead, already fumbling to light his second smoke.

"Don't look at me," he said. "I don't know anything."

3

"It wasn't here last night," Edie said.

"Duh." Hannah let her mouth hang open, smoke spilling out. She lifted one foot and knocked the peak off the little mountain of dirt at the edge of the hole. Edie peered down into the darkness. Hairy, gnarled roots poked out of damp earth cobwebbed with white threads of mycelia.

"Who was the last to leave?"

"Ask the rector." Hannah steepled her hands in a mockery of prayer and bowed toward Tuck. He pinched the cigarette against his lips.

"Me," he said. Not actually a rector in any official capacity, but he might as well have been. Always the first to arrive, always the last to leave. Edie sometimes wondered what he was avoiding. She had trouble checking the impulse to pry into everything. The Lump throbbed reproachfully. It did that now, when her journalistic ambitions got the better of her. She knew she was probably imagining it, but that—like the many statistics arguing in favor of its being entirely benign—did not comfort her much.

"Did you see anything weird?"

"Is this your first time here?" Hannah said. "Everything about this place is weird."

The Anchorite did seem oddly lost in time and space. It had stood on the same spot for two hundred years while the town and the college exploded around it. On one side, a parking garage cast a murky orange light, as if the night outside had oxidized. Glaring red letters spelled out EMERGENCY in the black sky southward. The west wall opened into an

4

alley behind the Calhoun Center for Behavioral Psychiatry, and the north wall followed a narrow road that eventually crossed paths with the modest nightlife flitting up and down Azalea Street. The light of the streetlamps encroached only so far, held at bay by a wall of ivy that had filled in the gaps between the bars of the fence. Within its crooked boundaries, angels wept elegantly over headstones while swinish gargoyles grinned and leered from their perches on either side of the church doors. Weeds grew without restraint. An oak tree even older than the church squatted in one corner, dropping acorns and orange leaves every October until the branches were bare and jack-o'-lantern mushrooms took up residence among the roots. Some had sprouted already, glowing eerily in the dark.

"I mean did you see anything man-made weird," Edie said. The hole clearly wasn't the work of an animal—the lines and angles too regular for paws and claws. "Tuck?"

He shook his head. "Nothing weirder than usual," he said. "No . . . hole."

Nobody wanted to call it what it obviously was, including Edie. She tugged her own pack of smokes from her pocket and struggled to get one lit. A cold breeze nipped at the tip of her nose and blew the flame out every time she spun the spark wheel.

"Here." Tuck opened his coat to offer temporary shelter from the elements.

"Thanks." She inhaled, exhaled, watched the smoke unfurl. "So, what do we do?"

"Do?" Tuck looked from her to Hannah. "Who says we have to do anything?"

"Do anything about what?"

They turned together toward the Drewalt obelisk, less startled than they might have been because they knew the voice.

"Tamar," Edie said, and breathed a little easier. Tamar was the oldest of the Anchorites, a sobering presence to counterbalance Tuck's twitchy agitation, Hannah's extravagant indifference.

"Hey," she said, emerging slowly from under the oak, cheeks dewy from her walk across campus from the Health Sciences Library. "How's ev— What's with the hole?"

"The very conundrum we were just contemplating," Hannah said, with a wry little smile.

Tamar looked her way, but Hannah only inhaled, exhaled, in Holmesian condescension. "Maybe there's a funeral this weekend," Tamar said, with a sigh, resigned to playing Watson for the moment. "Don't they dig beforehand if the ground is hard?"

Tuck shook his head. "Nobody's been buried here in a hundred years."

"And wouldn't you need a backhoe for that?" Edie asked. "I don't think they dig the old-fashioned way anymore."

"Maybe they do if they're trying to keep it real quiet," Hannah said, with ghoulish gravitas.

"Or," said Tamar, cooler head prevailing, "maybe somebody's just been disinterred."

"What *for?*" Tuck asked.

She shrugged. "Historical interest, maybe. It's an old church."

"Or dissection," Hannah suggested. "Don't they work on cadavers at the med school?"

"Yeah," Edie said. It was one of the few schools in the county to let premed students work on human bodies—a point of some controversy in her first year muckraking for the *Times*. Certain parents seemed to think it grotesque. "But I think they prefer them to be, uh, *fresh*."

Hannah flicked her first butt into the hole. They all leaned toward the center of the circle, watched it disappear. "Maybe," she said, "it's for somebody who's not dead yet."

"THE DARK LORD DEMANDS BLOOD SACRIFICE!"

Only Hannah was unsurprised. Tuck swore a blue streak; Tamar gasped and clutched her chest; Edie almost bit her tongue in half and dropped her cigarette in the dirt. She turned in fury toward the whispering oak. Theo Pavlopoulos came swashbuckling out of the shadows, but his laugh, like his name, preceded him—that deep, roguish chuckle that topped off every drink he poured at the Rocker Box Bar. *They hear his name and just start drooling*, or so the saying went. Wavy brown hair and black-coffee eyes, muscled like

Michelangelo's *David*. A textbook tall drink of your poison of choice.

"I think the Friar jumped right out of his robe," he observed, flashing his straight white teeth at Tuck. "Who's not dead yet?"

"You're lucky not to be," Tamar said darkly.

"Nine lives," Theo said, lighting up with the Zippo in his pocket. "And at least three left."

"Better start guarding them carefully," said Hannah. "Heard you had an 'Incident' in the Box." She angled a glance at Edie, who had, of course, supervised the coverage.

"Don't remind me."

"Who was it this time?" Tuck asked.

Edie already knew, but Edie listened. Wanting the story straight from the horse's mouth. She fished her cigarette out of the dirt, brushed off the filter, and pulled hard enough to keep the ember burning. The *Times*'s series on the Hostile Incidents afflicting the community since August had, so far, gone nowhere. Unless you counted going in circles. None of the Belligerents had anything in common. But at least the *Times* could claim credit for coining the terminology. Because nobody knew what it was or what to call it, they'd been forced to decide for themselves and spent most of a pitch meeting arguing over semantics.

Unbothered by such considerations, Theo shook his head, talked around the cigarette. He alone seemed immune to the cold inevitable after dark this deep into the year. Bareheaded and barehanded, he made no attempt to warm himself while the rest of them scuffed their feet and stuffed their fingers in their armpits. "Only knew him by sight. He hung out with the B-school crowd. Pretty buttoned-up until last night." The Rocker Box was the favored haunt of west campus, patronized mostly by the professional schools and undergraduates who had abandoned the dormitories for that drunken pastel blood sport known as Greek life. After the six years it took to work his way up to general manager, Theo knew enough dirty secrets to blackmail every department chair on campus and half the city council besides. Every night Edie barely resisted the temptation to pump him for information. It wouldn't have worked anyway; he treated the brass rail like a confessional, any admissions made there somehow sacrosanct. "Never knew him to have more than two drinks. Never even saw him drunk."

"Stone-cold sober to stone-cold crazy just like that, huh?" Hannah asked The Hole. She lit another cigarette, not with a lighter but with an old-fashioned matchbook. She flicked her wrist and the match went out, dragging a wisp of smoke behind it like a comet's tail.

"Well, I didn't have eyes on him all night." Theo took another pensive drag, barrel chest inflating like a bellows before he exhaled again. "But one minute he's drinking his Guinness, quiet as a mouse"—he smiled, inexplicably, at Tuck—"the next he's ranting and raving and smashing his head against the mirror in the men's room."

"That where you got the shiner?" asked Tamar. Edie squinted through the gloom, and the shadow under Theo's left eye resolved itself into a swollen black bruise.

"He put up a hell of a fight for a guy who wears a tie." As GM of the Rocker Box, Theo was one part bartender, one part business manager, one part one-man goon squad.

"I heard you crushed his trachea with your rippling biceps," Hannah said. She had a special talent for making a compliment sound like an insult. Theo redirected the grin across the open grave at her, unfazed.

"Nothing like a little light asphyxiation to calm a body down." The Pavlovian Chokehold had been deployed to such terrific effect over the years that nobody looking to keep their head attached to their neck got up to no good in the Box. Like the Pavlovian Charm, it tended to provoke excessive drooling.

"Watch what you say in front of Little Miss Woodward and Bernstein"—Hannah's eyes fastened on Edie—"or you'll find yourself on the front page tomorrow with all that suffocation and blood sacrifice taken out of context."

"Hey," Tamar said. "What happens in the graveyard stays in the graveyard."

"Sure about that?" Theo asked. He leaned over the side of The Hole. "Looks like there might be a dead man up and walking around somewhere."

"Or dead woman," Edie said, thinly. "Hannah looks a bit pale." So pale and gaunt she was downright cadaverous. Circles almost as dark as Theo's shiner hung under both her eyes.

"Me-yow," he said, and blew a smoke ring.

"Cut it out," said Tamar. "You all are worse than the students sometimes, honestly."

"I am a student," Edie reminded her.

"What did I do?" Tuck asked. Puffing and fidgeting, puffing and fidgeting.

"Did you dig The Hole?" Theo asked. "It's always the quiet ones."

"No, I did not dig The Hole." Tuck pulled his beanie a little lower over his ears. Embarrassed or annoyed or both. Tuck's every emotion manifested as a kind of nervous tic.

"So, who did?"

"We were just wondering that," Tamar said. "Before you interrupted." She turned back to Hannah. "What did you mean, it might be for somebody who's not dead yet?"

"Where better to bury the evidence? Nobody goes looking for a murder victim at the cemetery," she said. "If I were planning the perfect crime, I'd pick the plot beforehand, wouldn't you?"

"I love your sick mind," Theo said. "How are you still single?"

"Eat your heart out, Ivan."

"Sorry, I must have missed how we landed on murder," Tuck said.

"Occam's razor," said Tamar.

"Gesundheit," said Theo.

Tuck wisely ignored him. "Occam's what?"

"Occam's razor," Edie repeated. "The simplest explanation

11

is the best explanation." It was a motto she'd tried to instill in her staff at the *Times*—along with the official motto, *Salva veritate*. With truth intact. But the truth was never simple, seldom whole. She touched The Lump automatically. If Occam's razor had its way, she might have to have it and the larger lump of her left breast razored off. Goose bumps broke out up and down her arms.

"And murder is the simplest explanation why?" Tuck peered uneasily into The Hole.

"Can't be a legitimate interment because the church has been defunct for years," Edie recited. "Disinterment for medical research unlikely due to decay. Disinterment for historical research unlikely because, well, that would have been news, and I would have known." She knew she sounded like a know-it-all but had never figured out how to avoid that particular pitfall. She avoided Hannah's gaze instead.

"Maybe it's not news yet," Tuck said. "I mean, this can't have been dug before last night. We were all here, and no hole."

"Last night?" Theo said. "Can't have been dug more than about an hour ago."

"How do you know?" Edie asked, bracing herself for another idiotic joke. He and Hannah seemed utterly incapable of taking anything seriously.

Theo bent down, straightened up again with a handful of crumbling black earth. "The soil's still wet," he said, pressing it into a small, dense lump. Edie's fingers probed surreptitiously at The Lump beneath her arm again. Mortified she hadn't thought of that; astonished Theo had. He should have been dumber. Anybody that good-looking deserved to be dumb. "It hasn't rained for days," he added, brushing his hands off on his pants. "Whoever dug this did it very recently."

"Which means whoever dug this is probably coming back," Hannah said. "Probably soon."

"Well," Tamar said, and stubbed her cigarette out on the nearest headstone, "that's enough nightmares for me for one evening." She stuffed the butt into the small ornamental urn they had repurposed as an ashtray, nobody quite remembered how long ago. Full of ashes anyway, or so Hannah's reasoning went. The rest of them just went along. "Going to be up late as it is."

"Need a lift?" Hannah asked. "About time I clocked back in."

"Me too," Theo said, still rubbing his hands together, though most of the dirt had come loose. Staring off into the dark. "Can I—"

"You can walk." Hannah poked her cigarette into the urn, made a show of checking her watch. Raised her eyebrows. "Or maybe run." She vanished under the oak with a perfunctory backward glance at Tuck and Edie. "Let us know if Freddy Krueger comes to call."

Theo chuckled, dirty hands on his hips. "Such a fucking tease," he said, apparently to himself. Then, like Hannah, he spared one backward glance for Tuck and Edie. "Stick together, kids."

They watched him disappear after Hannah and Tamar. Stood on opposite sides of The Hole in awkward silence. Edie did not want to walk back to the *Times* office. Not without some answers, not without a story. For the first time since The Lump appeared, since her waking hours stretched and her sleeping hours shrank so dramatically, she felt wide awake. Murder or not, here was something worth investigating. She stubbed her cigarette out in the urn and turned her back on The Hole.

"Where are you going?" Tuck asked.

"To church," she said.

Edie would not go away. Tuck had tried to kill the conversation—something he usually managed to do without trying—but she was perfectly capable of playing both parts herself. Mostly posing rhetorical questions, thinking out loud, unable to leave the mystery of The Hole unresolved. She chattered at him as she crossed the churchyard, still moving insistently toward the Anchorite.

"Must be really hurting for news, huh?" he asked, risking outright rudeness in the hopes that she would finally relent, lose interest, and leave. Unlike the rest of them, he had nowhere to be and nowhere to go and was justifiably protective of the building. He'd been rationing his cigarettes, but under the circumstances considered another one justified. A fourth would be flirting with extravagance. He felt around his pockets for the pack, tripping over his own feet in his haste to catch up to her. She had a surprisingly long stride, weaving between headstones and weeping angels like it was some sort of nocturnal steeplechase.

"That obvious, huh?" she said, undeterred. "Everybody's lost interest in the Hostile Incidents." He could hear the capital letters. Wondered if she'd coined the term herself or simply gave it her editorial stamp of approval. "And there's not much else happening around here. Except this." She gestured over her shoulder at The Hole.

"Which is probably nothing." Was, in fact, nothing but negative space. Which didn't seem particularly newsworthy. Still, Edie was determined.

"Probably," she conceded. "But so far none of our simple explanations seems to fit."

"There must be something simple we haven't thought of."

"Probably," she said again. Then fell silent. He crossed his fingers in his pockets, hoping that meant she'd give up and go. But no, like a dog with a bone, she refused to let the matter drop. She jogged up the steps and stopped on the porch. The porcine gargoyles gaped down at her in silent, tongue-wagging hysterics. "When did you say this place was . . . decommissioned?"

"About a hundred years ago." He harbored a special loathing for the gargoyle on the left, which had a nose ring like a Spanish bull and eyes that seemed to follow you no matter where you stood. "Technically it's maintained by some historic preservation society, but they haven't done

much to preserve it besides keep the university from knock-
ing it down."

"Hm." The sign glared at them in the midnight gloom.
White letters on bare, mismatched boards. DANGER, KEEP
OUT. "Even a hundred years ago, I bet they kept a record of
everybody buried here."

"So what?"

"So, let's find out."

He pushed the door shut when she tried to pull it open.
"I don't think that's a good idea."

"Why not?"

He pointed to the sign. "You're the editor of the paper,
so I know you can read."

She rolled her eyes. "Yes, but can you *believe* everything
you read?"

"When a condemned building has a 'Danger, Keep Out'
sign on the door, I tend to believe it, yes."

"It's not condemned. You just said it's being 'preserved.'"

"I said it's being preserved from demolition, not that its
structural integrity has been preserved."

She wrinkled her nose, squinting suspiciously at him.
"Why do you know so much about it, anyway?"

He didn't have a good answer for that. He got tongue-
tied between unlikely excuses, and she took advantage of
his silence to push past him and heave the door open, DAN-
GER be damned. The hinges groaned, and a shaft of watery
moonlight threw itself down the aisle like a silver carpet.
"Coming?" Edie asked. He saw no way around it, silently

cursing her for being so curious and himself for being such a bad liar.

Their footsteps were muffled by a century's dirt and decay on the flagstone floor. The echo bouncing back from the modestly vaulted ceiling warped and wobbled, as if they were two scuba divers walking underwater. Edie tugged her gloves off to better navigate the touchscreen on her phone. The flashlight was more like a miniature floodlight, blooming through the dark of the nave until it climbed the wall behind the altar.

"Whoa." Edie stopped suddenly and Tuck walked right into her. She pointed the light up at the massive, weird mosaic of Saint Anthony. Paint had been applied directly to the plaster, embellished with shards of mirror and colored glass gems that glittered like the embers of a fire dying out—deep bloody reds and oxidized orange. The saint himself held, in one hand, a leash tethered to a stout, squatting creature that could have been a pig or an ugly hairless dog. In the other, he clutched an even uglier doll, with cabbage-like leaves sprouting out of its head. The doll had no hands or feet, but instead four hairy, rootlike protuberances where its hands and feet should have been. Which was not to say that there were no hands or feet at all. The most unsettling part of the icon was the half dozen disembodied hands and feet floating in midair above the hermit's head—a grotesque mobile of amputated limbs. "What is that thing?"

"Which thing?" There were so many to choose from. Edie pointed to the freaky, frondiferous doll.

"It's a mandrake," Tuck told her. "Physicians like the Antonines used them as a sedative for amputations." Saint Anthony stared down at them with mouth agape in speechless horror.

"Is that what all that's about?" Recovering from her shock somewhat, she directed the beam up at the severed hands and feet.

"Yeah. *Ignis sacer.*"

"Ignis what?"

"Saint Anthony's Fire. It was a sort of medieval epidemic. Caused gangrene and hallucinations and made people feel like they were being burned alive."

"What fun," Edie said. Her flashlight roved over the mosaic, illuminating the patches of pale greenish lichen creeping in from the corners and cracks in the plaster. The larger rosettes were starting to resemble ears of cauliflower. Tiny mushroom caps had popped out among the glass gems, dimly aglow with weird phosphorescence that reminded Tuck of the glow-in-the-dark stars stuck to the ceiling of his childhood bedroom. "Smells a bit like a pile of withered limbs in here, actually."

Tuck almost laughed. Damp and decay made the whole building feel like a mausoleum. "Fitting for old Saint Tony. He lived in a tomb for a while, or so says the lore."

Edie lowered her flashlight, looked away from the saint and back at Tuck instead. "Why do you know so much about this?" she asked again. He hadn't come up with a good answer since the first time she asked.

"'I collect spores, mold, and fungus,'" he said, nonsensically.

"What?"

"Microbiology." He neglected to mention he'd never finished the degree. Couldn't afford the loans. Had already defaulted on the payments, already accrued late fees and interest, already been reported as a financial delinquent to all the credit bureaus. "Mycology, really. Saint Anthony's Fire was just another name for ergot poisoning."

"I hate to admit it," Edie said, "but Hannah's right. This place is deeply fucking weird."

"You wanted to come in here," he said.

"And you've clearly been in here before," she said, with a flicker of a smile. Found out. "So, where do you think they keep the burial records?"

He sighed, resigning himself to the search. Cooperating with her inquisition seemed easiest, and Tuck—worn down by years of debt and drudgery—often opted for the path of least resistance. "The office upstairs," he said. "Come on, it's this way." He led her down the aisle, toward the rickety spiral staircase at the back of the nave. "Careful. That third step is tricky."

He hadn't warned her soon enough. She slipped, grabbed his shoulder, and almost pulled him over backward. "Sorry," she said, whispering now, the funereal hush of the Anchorite getting the better of her. He didn't need the flashlight. Knew the steps by heart.

"You wanted danger," he said. "Watch your head." At the top of the stairs, a wall sconce had come loose and fallen across the walkway. Edie ducked underneath and kept close behind him, following like a shadow. The corridor dead-ended at another oak door, which moaned mournfully when he threw his shoulder against it, the hinges crusted over with rust. None of the electric lights worked, but there were plenty of white tapers in a box that had been mostly protected from the elements. He lit the two in the candelabra on the desk, which cast just enough light to read by. A stained glass window on the west wall transformed the moonlight to a swirl of watercolor. "Okay," Tuck said, "knock yourself out." He backed into the corner, shuffling his feet, trying to nudge the backpack and sleeping bag crumpled there deeper into the dark. Edie was already busy pulling the bookshelves apart. There was surprisingly little dust. Too much moisture. Each volume fell open to reveal enormous water spots, some even growing mold where the papers met the pasteboard.

Smoking in a room so full of books had never seemed a good idea, but nothing was dry enough to catch, really, and Tuck needed another smoke to smooth his fraying nerves. They'd thrown caution to the wind already, so why not? He tugged his gloves off, shook a cigarette out of the pack, and leaned forward to light it by the taller candle's flame. Fuck the ration. The night had taken too many strange turns to worry about how he'd pay for smokes tomorrow. Maybe the unnecessary expense would finally force him to quit. He puffed quietly, ignoring Edie and watching out the window. The Hole was a long, dark void in the graveyard below.

"What's this?"

He looked her way. "Find something?"

"Not what I was looking for, but—is this yours?"

Tuck's heart dropped into his stomach like an elevator car in free fall. He'd forgotten the journal—the battered field notebook he'd filled with jottings and sketches and still occasionally leafed through, doodled in. She'd picked it up off the desk and opened the cover, and there was his name, blurred and water-stained like everything else, but it said, unmistakably, in his clumsy childish writing, *Wes Tucker.*

"Guess I must have left it," he said. Sucking on the cig-arette to play for time, wishing he had a better poker face. Any poker face at all. "Sometimes I sketch in here."

"Is that it?" She was looking past him, not at him. Had spotted the sleeping bag and the backpack kicked halfway out of sight. "What's with the sleeping bag?"

He flicked his ash into the opposite corner. The books were too waterlogged to hold a flame, but he wasn't sure about the nylon and couldn't afford to set fire to his few worldly possessions. "Just needed a roof over my head for a while," he said. "Didn't see the harm. Except for you, nobody has ever ignored the 'Danger' sign."

She was silent for a moment, straight dark hair casting half her face in shadow. "Theo knows, doesn't he?" she said, which was not what he expected her to say.

"Unfortunately," Tuck admitted. "How did *you* know he knew?" He was learning not to underestimate her investigative instincts.

"All the . . . names." She shrugged, looking embarrassed on his behalf. "Churchmouse. Friar Tuck."

"Yeah."

"What a world-class dickhead," she said.

He smirked in spite of himself. "No comment."

"Did you tell him?"

"Do I look like an idiot? He saw me come out, a few weeks back."

"Weeks?" She shifted her feet, biting her lip. "That seems . . . I mean, look at the mold in here. There are probably bats in the belfry. Never mind ergot, you could get mold poisoning. You could get rabies."

"Right, well, it wasn't my first choice," he said. "I ran out of options and need somewhere to sleep while I figure things out."

"I don't mean to pry, b—"

"There's no story here, okay?" he said, more sharply than he should have. "I'm broke. I'm squatting. That's it." One of the candles guttered and sputtered, melting down into the bracket.

"I wasn't looking for a story," she said. Voice shrinking at the accusation. "I'm just—I don't know, what would you say, if it were me?"

He blinked at her across the desk. The candlelight dying down to a murmur. "I try not to be a dickhead, but I'm not trying to be a hero either," he told her. "I wouldn't say anything."

She blinked back at him. Seemed at a loss for words at first, then gasped, "Tuck!"

"Jesus, could you drop it?"

"No, Tuck, *look*." She backed against the bookcase, vanishing from the narrow beam of light slanting in from the window. *"There's someone in the graveyard."*

He flattened himself against the wall. Practiced, by now, at sliding out of sight when anybody went by, just in case. "Could be Theo," he said. "Or Hannah, coming back."

Edie shook her head vigorously. "Too short to be Theo, too broad to be Hannah."

And too dark to see much else. "Put the candle out."

Edie's arm darted forward and with a soft *hiss* the flame turned to smoke. Tuck squinted down at the ground. It was difficult to make out much but Rorschach blots in the shape of a person. Probably a man, maybe—a hunchback? "What is that?" he breathed, though it was unlikely the interloper could see them through the colored glass, less likely still that he could hear them.

"He's carrying something," Edie whispered. "It looks . . . heavy."

"Not heavy enough for whatever you're thinking." Tuck came away from the wall, squatted down to squint through a hole in the window where a couple of panes had popped out. Wind whistled through the gap at night, letting the outside in. No matter in the last warm gasp of September, but this far into October, the cold cut to the bone.

"What's he doing?"

"Shh." He held his breath, watching and waiting for—what? The dark figure below lowered the bag from his shoulder. Like a sinister, necromantic Santa Claus. "He's, uh, unloading."

"Unloading *what?*" The whisper tickled the back of his ear and he nearly jumped through the window.

"Don't scare me like that!" He hadn't even heard her move, but he could feel her now, crouching right behind him.

"Sorry."

"*Shh.*"

The gravedigger looked around—glancing first toward the parking deck, then toward the Calhoun Center. He turned the bag upside down. Whatever was in it tumbled out into The Hole in pieces. "Oh God," Tuck muttered. Head suddenly spinning—a glittering, gruesome whirl of disembodied arms and legs, hands and feet. "I think I might be sick."

"*Shhh!*" Edie's turn to shush him. She grabbed his collar and pulled him away from the glass. "*He's still out there, Tuck, shut up!*" He obediently clamped his eyes and mouth shut. Let her take the lead. Let her handle it. He wasn't a dickhead, wasn't a hero, and didn't care if he was a coward. For what felt like a lifetime, they stayed there. Not moving, not breathing, though Edie's grip on his collar was growing uncomfortably tight.

"He's going," she said. "He's leaving, he's walking back toward—which way did he come from?"

"I don't know, I didn't see—"

"Looks like he's going down the alley—"

"Edie—"

"Of course that doesn't mean that's the direction he came from—"

"Edie! You're choking me."

"Oh." She released him. "Oh, I'm sorry. Oh no, he's gone."

"Oh *no?*"

"Come on."

"What?"

"Come on!"

"Come where? Down *there?* Are you nuts?" It was the first time he could remember feeling rather cozy in the Anchorite office, feeling rather reluctant to leave it. But Edie was on her feet and out the door, undaunted by darkness and gravediggers. "O-kay," he said to himself, finding himself abruptly alone. "Evidently yes. Evidently nuts." He stood up from the floor. Looked around the musty room. Then, not knowing what else to do, started after her. "Evidently both of us. Evidently I am also completely *fucking* nuts."

When he poked his head out between the front doors, wincing as the hinges whined, Edie was standing with her back turned, staring down into The Hole. Because she wasn't running or screaming or in pieces on the ground, he ventured farther out. "Edie? What is it?"

She started, looked toward his voice, as if he'd just shaken her out of a dream. "Tuck, I don't know what it is."

"Not, like, a body?" He felt like an idiot now, saying it out loud.

"Not *a* body, no," she said, and he heard it then—the edge of unease. "It's a *lot* of bodies."

"Excuse me, it's *what?*"

"Not human bodies! Just come look. Or—I don't know, how squeamish are you?"

"'I collect spores, mold, and fungus,'" he said again. Trying to convince himself that he wasn't such a coward after all. He shuffled closer, looked over Edie's shoulder, and saw a lot of bodies. A lot of small furry bodies with long spiderweb whiskers and scaly pink tails. Dozens of white furry bodies with little black hoods. Like a mass grave for tiny monks after some religious massacre. "Are those . . . rats?"

"Too big to be mice," Edie said.

"What's wrong with them?" They were all dead, stiff in the grip of rigor mortis, mouths gaping to show their sharp yellow teeth. Tuck had lived in more than his fair share of shitholes, was no stranger to the sight of dead rodents. But their eyes were wide open—each one frozen in that attitude of paralyzed surprise.

"Don't ask me, I barely survived one semester of biology." Edie glanced toward the red light in the black sky that screamed EMERGENCY. "Maybe they're lab rats. They don't look like vermin, not with that coloring."

"I survived enough biology to know this is not the protocol for disposing of dead laboratory animals." At least he'd learned something from his abortive attempts to become a real mycologist. "They have . . . bags and freezers and incinerators for that sort of thing."

"Yeah," Edie said. "I'll bet they do." The anxiety had evaporated. She pulled her phone from her pocket again, fumbling around until the flash went off like a fork of lightning.

"What the hell are you doing?" Tuck glanced toward the alleyway where the gravedigger had disappeared.

"Gathering information."

Another flash. Then a third. The screen illuminated her face from below as she flicked through the photos, as if she were about to tell a fireside ghost story.

"All right, I'm sure you got their good side," Tuck told her. "Would you knock it off?"

"Why? Can't h—"

"*Because he's coming back.*"

Tuck grabbed her elbow and dragged her behind the nearest headstone tall and wide enough to hide them. He landed on all fours and let go when he felt her hands and knees hit the ground beside him. They stayed low, watching in stricken silence as the gravedigger's shadow advanced along the wall, then slipped out of sight behind the Drewalt obelisk. His footsteps were slightly uneven, with a hitch and a scrape, a hitch and a scrape. The man in the flesh emerged, dragging a shovel behind him.

He paused at the edge of The Hole. Looked one way, then the other, his features swallowed up in shadow. All Tuck could make out was a long coat with buttons and the scruffy silhouette of a beard. He turned his back again, angled the shovel into the mound of earth Theo had pawed through half an hour ago, and dug in.

Tuck pressed his back flat against the headstone, clenched his fists so tight he lost feeling in his fingertips. Edie craned her neck as far as she dared, straining for a glimpse of the gravedigger at work. Tuck had no desire to watch, no desire to listen. He shut his eyes tight against the hideous crunch of the shovel blade in the dirt, the scattering of soil over the cold, scabrous mass of dead rats. Their little pink feet clenched like talons, scaly tails forever entangled. His stomach churned. *Crunch. Crunch. Crunch.*

How long did it take to fill a shallow grave? His hands were numb and his knees were beginning to ache from squatting there like one of the churchyard gargoyles. Edie vibrated like a tuning fork beside him, itching to catch the gravedigger in the act or just too excited to sit still. Her foot kept twitching against his leg. Afraid the gravedigger might hear her sneaker chafe against his jeans, Tuck opened his eyes to try to mime at her to *Stop, just fucking stop!* but when he did, she wasn't touching him. Wasn't even close. Still down on all fours, ignoring him completely as she maneuvered for a better view around the tombstone, hair hanging over her shoulder so she looked headless in the dark. That might have alarmed him, but something touched his leg again and a wild terror jumped down his throat.

He kicked out violently, but the rat's claws had hooked into his jeans like Velcro. Edie elbowed him hard, elbowed him again when he didn't stop squirming, and finally turned. Tuck's tortured expression—face screwed up with effort as he tried not to whimper, straining as far as away from those needling claws as he could in the shadow of the headstone—made her look down at his knees and recoil. The rat was climbing his leg, climbing his body, nosing toward his groin with demented determination.

Crunch. Crunch. Crunch.

He jiggled his leg, but it only climbed faster. He snapped and grabbed the rat to fling it off, but it squealed like a piglet and bit at his fingers, and the crunch of the shovel suddenly stopped. The gravedigger straightened up. Tuck sat still as a stone, hands closed fast around the struggling rat, squeezing its tiny head in his fist to stifle the squealing. It gnawed and scratched against his grip, and he would have screamed if not for Edie, who'd stuffed her loose glove in his mouth. He ground his teeth into the leather.

The gravedigger's head turned again—this way and that. Listening. Hearing nothing but the nocturnal rustlings of the Anchorite's backyard. The breeze through the dead oak leaves, the occasional uncanny titter of the screech owls that lived in the tree trunk. The distant guttural noise of car engines on Azalea Street. He lowered the shovel, working faster now.

Crunch, crunch, crunch.

Tuck had started to cry, but the rat had stopped struggling. Grip loose, neck limp. Head like a soft, rotten walnut in the hollow of his palm. One foot twitched feebly, and he almost threw up in his lap.

Crunch, crunch, crunch.

Tuck must have astral-projected out of his body. Left it just like the rat, but only temporarily. When the rhythmic swing of the shovel slowed, he came back to himself with an awful, vertiginous plunge. The gravedigger's labored breath rattled in the thin air. He smoothed the earth flat with the back of the shovel, then kicked some leaves and twigs and other detritus over the looser ground. He looked around again and, seeing no shadow but his own on the wall, took the shovel and slunk out of the churchyard.

Tuck spat out Edie's glove and dropped the dead rat in the grass. When the gravedigger's footsteps faded out of earshot, she darted across four or five plots to the gate and peered out. "He went left," she muttered. "Around the corner toward downtown."

"Spectacular," Tuck said. "Except he forgot this." He climbed to his feet, turned the rat over with the toe of his shoe. Unsure whether he'd broken its neck or squeezed the life right out of it in sheer, stupid panic. He hadn't meant to kill it, but looking down at it now, he couldn't help feeling he'd done it a favor. "Bring that light over here."

Edie's phone threw a wide circle of antiseptic white. Under its glare it was easy to imagine the rat in a lab—unseamed with a scalpel, viscera untangled, pinned down and labeled. Its fur had fallen out in patches, the skin underneath scratched raw and stretched grotesquely over a jumble of bones with no fat or muscle on them. A fibrous white crust had gathered around its nostrils and in the corners of its eyes and mouth.

"Maybe you do need a rabies shot," Edie said, glancing down at his hands. The skin was already red and tender, bites and scratches oozing blood.

"It's not foaming," he said. "It looks more like . . . huh. I don't know." But it did look familiar. Scaly and flaky and producing pale curling filaments almost too fine to see. Edie gasped again, but this time he wasn't even startled, his whole nervous system blue-screened and blank.

"I do!" she said. And the flashlight ran off.

"Of course you do," Tuck muttered, resigned to following after her again. The church doors groaned, and he trudged up the steps. Edie's flashlight led him through the narthex and into the nave again. Saint Anthony gazed balefully down at them, but he didn't seem to be the object of Edie's attention. The flashlight bounced back and forth across the mosaic until it settled in the top left corner, above one of the gangrenous feet.

"There!" she said. "Do you see that?" A chalky whitish

growth had sprouted from a wet spot on the ceiling, the larger patches starting to form curling rosettes edged with green.

He didn't want to, but he did. "Edie, that's just lichen."

"So?"

"So, lichens grow on static substrates—rocks, trees, walls. They don't normally grow on, uh, soft tissues." He wasn't sure which was worse, the memory of the rat's twisting body or of its limp, unmoving one.

"Well, like Hannah said"—she snapped a few new pictures—"nothing about this is normal." She lowered the phone, typing furiously. "And it's the best lead we have." She thumbed through the photos, which gave her face a sallow greenish glow.

"Lead?" he said. "Who are you expecting to investigate?"

"Let's think, who's up at this hour and would just jump at the chance to join Mystery Inc.?"

Tuck sighed. "Oh, no."

Thursday night at the Rocker Box was not rocking, exactly, but was still going strong one hour from closing. Behind the bar Theo and his right-hand drink-slinger mixed cocktails and pulled pints and closed tabs with ambidextrous efficiency. A good thing, too, since the rest of his first string had taken time off to recover from the shock of their "Hostile Incident." It hadn't kept patrons away, which kept him and Chelsea busy. Also a good thing, because—in a moment of temporary insanity he blamed entirely on Jack Daniel's and holiday cheer at last year's Christmas shindig—he'd broken his rule about not sleeping with coworkers. There had been a few more flare-ups of temporary insanity before yesterday, when he had, in her estimation, "overreacted" to the flirtatious overtures of a good-looking med student haunting her end of the bar. Oddly, insisting that he would have done the same for any of his staff under the circumstances, when a Hostile Incident might just walk through the door and order a drink, only seemed to make her angrier. Their conversation since was reduced to the logistical shorthand of food service:

"Corner!"

"Eighty-six the poppers."

"Behind."

"Coming in hot."

"Five out, hangover mac."

"Corner!"

Because the Rocker Box was the only bar on west campus to serve food until closing, they kept busy until two and didn't get home until four, if they went home at all. Theo had been short-staffed for so long that some nights he was too tired to climb the stairs to his apartment and slept sitting up in the corner booth.

He was starting to itch for a cigarette. Nicotine was the only thing that kept his mind sharp after working so many nights in a row, but he couldn't leave Chelsea alone at the bar again. She'd been glaring daggers at him all night.

"CORNER!"

He turned around with a Jack and Coke in each hand, lost his grip, and threw the drinks all over her and the baskets of wings she was holding. Cola dripped from the end of her ponytail. A couple of people at the bar stifled snickers. Theo threw the glasses in the bin—empty anyway—took the baskets from her hands, and slid them down the bar. Fuck it.

"Hey, this has somebody's drink all over it."

"No, that's our new Coca-Cola barbecue sauce, sweet and tangy, trust me, you'll love it," Theo told him, and steered Chelsea into the kitchen, muttering apologies. "I'm sorry, you hate me, I know, I'll make it right, let's just get through tonight—"

"I don't know, can you restrain yourself if I go back out there as a walking wet T-shirt contest?" She threw her arms wide, white shirt clinging to her body like wallpaper.

"Shit," he said. "I'm sorry, I'm an asshole, I'll get it cleaned. Or just get you a new one. Let me go grab you something to wear." He started up the back stairs.

"Don't bother guarding my virtue," she called after him. "I could use the tips!"

He couldn't afford to lose her as a bartender, didn't want to lose her as a . . . whatever else they were to each other. He'd grovel if she wanted groveling, but he couldn't figure out *what* she wanted. A problem for another night. Tonight had enough problems, one of which was that he hadn't done laundry in who knew how long. He rummaged through the mountain of shit on the bed, then through the mountain of shit in the closet. He found nothing there, then remembered the old Rocker boxing robes they'd made for the staff to wear on Halloween three years ago. He yanked his off the hanger, grabbed a half-eaten granola bar off the sofa in the back room, and stuffed it in his mouth. He hadn't eaten anything since breakfast but random french fries and hush puppies filched out of baskets waiting in the kitchen. As he chewed, his phone buzzed where it was plugged in on the end table. He picked it up, surprised to see a text from Edie. Just to him, not the group.

GRAVEDIGGER INCOMING, the first line read. He scrolled through the rest as he thumped down the stairs. He watched Chelsea throw back a shot with the cook, Noah, then handed her the robe. "A promotion?" she said, with a bright, fake smile. "For me?"

"Promotion?" Noah looked from her to Theo with a frown. Nobody had gotten a promotion or a raise for two years—Theo included. Kids just didn't drink like they used to.

"Yeah." She rammed her arms through the sleeves. "I've been upgraded from wet T-shirt to *Memoirs of a Geisha*."

"Really sorry, Chels," Theo said, again. "I'll make it up to you," he said, again. Though he had no idea how, especially since he was about to make everything much worse. "I gotta step out for a minute. Think you guys can hold the fort? Thanks." He didn't wait for an answer, didn't wait around to wither under The Glare. He slipped out the back door without even stopping to put on a coat.

GRAVEDIGGER INCOMING, Edie had written. *Walking up Dogwood, long coat, bearded, with shovel (?).* Sent three minutes ago. If he hustled, maybe he could intercept him. And do . . . what? He'd figure that out on the way, he decided, and picked up the pace. He knew better than to run flat out, with no coat on in the cold. He jogged down the long alley behind the bar, which spat him out at the deserted intersection of Dogwood and Azalea. He turned right and continued down the side street, where a few cars were parked in the gritty pink light of the few anemic streetlamps. One, he noticed, was parked farther down the block, away from the others, hiding in the shadows of an enormous magnolia that leaned drunkenly over the sidewalk.

"Where would I park if I was up to no good?" he asked himself, downshifting to a slower jog. Really more of a trot. Picking his feet up higher than he needed to, taking shorter strides than came naturally. Nothing to see here, just a fellow out for some fresh air in his T-shirt at one in the morning. Then, around the corner Theo himself had turned on his way back to the bar from the graveyard, came a man in a long overcoat. Too far to see if he had a beard or a shovel. Only one way to find out, Theo reasoned, and kept trotting along. The man in the coat made a beeline for the car parked under the magnolia—a shitty, half-rusted Honda Whatever from some year before he was born. The kind of car driven by adjuncts, dropouts, and Hannah. He'd convinced her to give him a ride once or twice, and once or twice invited her up to the apartment. In retrospect, sleeping with Hannah was even crazier than sleeping with coworkers, just because *she* was crazy. Never a fucking he forgot in a hurry, even if she was gone when he woke up in the morning, like she'd never been there at all.

The man with the coat walked slowly, dragging his feet. Or maybe a shovel. Theo didn't see what it was, but he watched him unlock the trunk, heave something inside, and slam it shut again. He saw Theo coming toward him and hurried to unlock the driver's door. The car was so old he had to do it the old-fashioned way, jamming the key in the lock and rattling it around until it turned. Theo jogged on, past the car and slowly down the street. The door slammed. He jogged a little farther, muscles shrinking from the cold. He heard the engine sputter and stall, sputter and stall. The third time it tried to turn over, it made a nasty snarling noise and then fell silent. Well, well.

Theo turned at the end of the street, trotted back the way he came. The best approach was a direct approach. At least, the best approach was a direct approach when you were six three and reasonably confident in your ability to throw half a dozen drunken frat rats out of your bar every weekend. His knee had started to ache, though—an unpleasant reminder of Tuesday's Hostile Incident and the fact that he was no longer twentysomething and invincible. The Belligerent should have given him no trouble—scrawny and bespectacled and wearing a *suit*, for Chrissake—but he'd kicked and screamed like a man possessed until Theo pinned him against the bar in a one-armed chokehold and held him there until he passed out. Thinking better of his boldness, Theo slowed his pace, approached the gravedigger more cautiously.

The Honda Whatever had evidently given up the ghost.

The dome light was on, but the engine was cold. The grave-digger sat in the driver's seat, slumped over the wheel, still loosely clutching the key in the ignition. Theo knocked lightly on the window. The man started in alarm and Theo opened his hands to show they were empty. Realizing a moment too late that his rancid black eye might be slightly alarming, he gave the gravedigger a winning smile until he cranked the window down.

"Car trouble?" he asked. "Sorry to startle you. Thought maybe I could help."

The man ran his hand through his hair. Scratched his beard. "Thanks," he said, "but not sure how you can." He looked about forty but might have looked younger without the dark circles under both eyes. *Hey, we match!* seemed the wrong thing to say, so Theo didn't mention it. He nodded down the street toward civilization, the red light at the intersection with Azalea.

"If somewhere warm to wait for a tow and a drink to drown your sorrows might help, it's on the house." He didn't know whether the gravedigger would recognize him. Most people who hung around west campus did. He might have even served this man a drink before; he only remembered the regulars and rabble-rousers anymore.

The gravedigger hesitated. Rubbed his knuckles into his eyes as if that might wake him up from this particular bad dream. When he opened them again and saw nothing had changed, he sighed. "All right. Might not help, but it probably wouldn't hurt."

"That's the spirit," Theo told him. "Walk this way."

The gravedigger climbed out of the car and locked it again after a lot of fussing and fidgeting. It didn't seem worth breaking into, but what did Theo know? The man had secrets. What man didn't? He decided to reserve judgment—then realized, with tingle of unease, that Edie hadn't said how she knew this man was the gravedigger. Maybe Theo would have to do some digging of his own.

They walked briskly, hands in their pockets, making small talk about the bar, the car, what had changed around town over the years and what hadn't. The gravedigger had been there almost as long as Theo had, by the sound of it.

"Been to the Rocker Box before?" He held the door open for a blast of warm air and loud conversation to come out into the cold.

"Ah, don't think so," the gravedigger said. "Don't get out much. I work late, most nights."

"What kind of work?" Theo asked. But his companion was understandably distracted by the damp-drying blonde in the red silk robe behind the bar. Chelsea looked up from the POS terminal just in time to watch Theo and his new friend walk in. Confusion and fury clashed in her expression, and while the gravedigger was busy ogling her—less lecherous than bewildered, like he wasn't quite sure whether he might, in fact, be dreaming—Theo did undignified charades behind his back. Trying to signal, *Be cool, I got this, I owe you, I'm sorry I'm such a bastard.* She shook her head, The Glare back with such a vengeance he thought he might turn to stone on the spot, then whirled away, slamming a check down in front of its owner with undue violence. "Usually she's charming," Theo said, only when he was absolutely certain she was absolutely out of earshot. "I threw a drink on her earlier and she hasn't forgiven me yet. Here, have a seat." He waved the gravedigger onto the stool at the lonelier end of the bar. "What's your poison?"

"Dealer's choice."

"I was hoping you'd say that." Theo reached for a mixing glass. "Mind if I see some ID? Have to ask in case you're an undercover cop—can't afford to lose my liquor license."

"Sure, sure." The gravedigger dug around the inside pocket of his coat and handed over a card. Theo glanced at it, handed it back.

"Gonna need something with your age on it, bud."

"Oh." He replaced his student ID and gave Theo his driver's license instead. "Sorry."

"They got you working with your hands this time of night?" Theo asked.

The gravedigger looked down, noticed in the dim light of the bar the dirt under his fingernails, the dark residue of the soil pressed into the fine lines of his palms. He cleared his throat. "Pest control. Easier in these university buildings when they're empty."

"I'll bet," Theo said, and pointed toward the back. "Bathroom's that way if you want to wash up."

"Right," he said, and slipped off the stool. "Yeah. Thanks."

Theo watched him wade through the crowd, then turned his back on the rest of the customers and whipped his phone out of his pocket. It had been buzzing against his butt cheek like a swarm of fucking bees since they walked into the bar. Thirty unread messages, all on the group text called Anchorites. He scrolled through half a dozen variations of *omg* and *WTF??* from Tamar and a deadpan *Looks delicious* from Hannah before he hit the picture. Sent, of course, by Edie. He almost dropped the phone. "Wow. I guess that's one way of doing pest control." He'd seen rats before, but not like that.

"I can think of a couple of pests I'd like to get under control." Chelsea elbowed past him to get to the grenadine. "If you're not going to help me while your date is here, could you *at least* get out of my way?"

She didn't seem to need an answer, which was just as well because he was fresh out. All he had were more questions. But he knew someone in the question-and-answer business. He speed-scrolled back to the bottom of the thread and butted in to say, *Not caught up with this, but caught up to this guy.* He glanced toward the bathroom, snapped a picture of the gravedigger's ID, and hit send. He tucked the phone back in his pocket and reached for the vermouth.

When the gravedigger returned, Theo passed his ID and a frosted highball glass across the bar. "Try that on for size," he said, conveniently forgetting to mention that he'd made the drink three times its usual size. Trusting the gravedigger not to know any better.

"What is it?" he asked.

Theo leaned on the bar on his elbows, lowered his voice. "We call that the Corpse Reviver." The gravedigger's left eye gave a gratifying little twitch. He leaned back again. "Of course that's the Pavlopoulos Variation on the Corpse Reviver #1." Back to business. Ignoring his phone, vibrating nonstop in his pocket. "Not as popular as the #2, but it makes a better nightcap."

The gravedigger gulped more than sipped, which was exactly what Theo wanted him to do. He'd made the drink longer, stronger, and sweeter than it had any right to be. Wanted it to go down easy. "That's nice, yeah."

"Glad to hear it."

"Mirror's broken in your bathroom, by the way," said the gravedigger. Another gulp. He wiped his beard with a cocktail napkin. Hands a little unsteady already, if Theo wasn't imagining it. "Supposed to be bad luck."

"Believe me, it was."

"What happened?"

"I don't know if you've been following the news," Theo said. Already starting to mix another drink. If he kept the conversation going, he could replace the empty glass with a full one and the gravedigger might not even notice. Like Indiana Jones, trading a sack of sand for a priceless golden icon. "We had a Hostile Incident, a couple of days ago."

The gravedigger set the glass down slowly. "Yeah, I think I heard something about that. Fuzzy on the details, though."

"You and me both," Theo said. But he'd told the story

so many times that by now it was almost routine. "He sat just about where you are. Regular customer, pretty unobtrusive until Tuesday. About midnight he's nodding over his drink like he's about to fall asleep. Gets up and heads to the bathroom. Dr. Jekyll goes in. He's in there a while. Somebody knocks on the door, and *bang*." He smacked one hand on the bar, just to watch the gravedigger jump. "Mr. Hyde comes out. Howling. Howling like—I don't know. Not a sound I've ever heard a human being make. Swinging at everyone and everything in swinging distance. Not just with his fists either—this guy was out for blood. Trying to sink his teeth in people."

The gravedigger swirled his drink around, tugged at his collar as it if were too tight. "What set him off?"

"You know, I've been asking myself that for two days. Or my three cracked ribs have been asking."

The gravedigger laughed, reluctantly. "Hope you get hazard pay."

Theo shrugged. "Goes with the territory. You really want to see some carnage, come back on Halloween." He smiled. Charm itself. Nudged another drink across the bar. "Or hey, maybe I'll call you . . . if I need another pest removed."

Unlike the library circulation desk, which was nonstop action around midterm season, the hotel reception desk was nonstop doldrums. It was one of the better hotels in town, and catered to visiting speakers, visiting parents, and visiting student-athletes. None of them likely to check in during Tamar's shift, leaving her little to do but answer the phones, which rarely rang, leaving her plenty of time to scroll through her own between games of solitaire on the antique IBM desktop. During the first few weeks of her tenure there, she'd whiled away the hours filling her educational history into job application portals, which had already asked her to upload a CV with all the same information, in the hopes of getting a job with actual tenure.

One year, one divorce, and exactly one tenure-track interview later, she'd given up on doing anything more exciting with her library science degree than menial data entry and occasionally reorganizing her rickety bookshelves according to a different classification system. She'd already grown bored with Dewey Decimal and Library of Congress and was considering a foray into the Universal Decimal system just for something to do. Not that she had the energy to do much of anything between her two jobs and what she suspected was major depressive disorder with melancholic features. She was not a doctor, and the only doctors in her network who could have made a formal diagnosis had waiting lists so long she was about as likely to get an appointment as she was to get a job with better health insurance. But since she transferred to the Health Sciences Library to shorten her commute from one desk to the next, she'd taken to flipping through the DSM-5 out of morbid curiosity. Wondering which Venn diagram of diagnostic codes might apply to her, her parents and siblings, her ex-wife.

Lately, she'd even embarked on armchair diagnoses of the few people she still thought of as friends, including the Anchorites. Edie seemed an obvious candidate for generalized anxiety disorder. Tuck, maybe a mild case of avoidant personality disorder. Theo seemed to be annoyingly neurotypical except for the nicotine addiction and sleep-wake dysfunction they all had in common. While the rest of them could blame their nocturnal tendencies on obvious external factors, only Hannah seemed to meet the criteria of a true insomniac. Maybe with a streak of sociopathy, but her un-flinching indifference to everything could be a side effect of perpetual sleep deprivation. She never slept, so far as Tamar could tell, and Tamar was the only other Anchorite to spend a whole night with her. So far as she knew.

Hannah's response to the hysterics in the group text was predictably toneless. *A rousing success for the campus composting initiative.* Tamar could have done without the extreme close-up of the dead rat Theo had already chris-tened "Tuck Jr." A leprose white substance had accumu-lated in its ears, mouth, and nose. But the eyes were the most disturbing, each shiny black bead crusted over with pale, ulcerous . . . sores? Spores? She couldn't tell from the photo, sent not from Edie but from Tuck's prehistoric flip phone. A second photo had followed, this one of a huge, weird mural supposedly depicting Saint Anthony. *Looks like the same stuff?* Edie had asked. Tamar didn't know what she meant. It just looked like a Boschian nightmare to her. But the third photo came from Theo, along with the question *Tamar, anybody you recognize?*

She stared at it, hard. The ID belonged to a man named Tom Kinnan. Five ten, brown hair, brown eyes, thirty-four years old, sporting a ducktail beard that did not flatter his face. "Tom Kinnan . . ." she said. He did look familiar, but she wasn't sure why Theo had asked her specifically until she realized—he was a student. Or perhaps, like her, contin-gent faculty. It didn't matter. She knew now exactly where she'd seen him.

Yes! she wrote back. She let the phone clatter down on the desk and swiveled back to the monitor. She closed out of her solitaire game and opened a new browser tab. She couldn't access library user information from an external terminal, but if Kinnan had published anything—and at thirty-four he was probably a grad student or an adjunct, so he probably had—she could find him.

While she waited for the page to load, she listed everything she could remember about Tom Kinnan from her time behind the circulation desk. He had a new pile of books to drop off or collect every week. He worked late, and early, and always had a cup of coffee in his hand, which always seemed to be fighting a losing battle against the bags under his eyes. A feeling Tamar knew all too well, which was partly why he lingered in her mind.

Once the old computer decided to cooperate, she pulled up the university directory, and soon she was scrolling through his departmental profile page. PhD candidate in psychiatry, research assistant to Dr. Heather Lockley, who had an office at the Calhoun Center. Undergrad at Penn, MS at Rutgers. His areas of interest included circadian rhythm and endocrine disorders, systems biology, complementary and alternative medicine. She clicked on the Publications tab and found a long list of articles, mostly coauthored with Lockley, their titles too clogged with technical jargon for Tamar to make much sense of them. The most recent one was about "Hypnotic and Antispasmodic Properties of *C. burranicum* Alkaloids." She scrolled a little farther, jotting down key vocabulary on the pad of hot-pink Post-it notes at her elbow. When she reached the bottom of the page, she closed out of the directory and logged into her library account.

After trying and failing to find a better job, trying and failing to make her marriage work, trying and failing to give up smoking, trying and failing to take care of herself as she sank into the quicksand of depressive lethargy, Tamar had come to think of herself, generally, as a failure. Her only real talent was tracking down elusive information. It started in a high school computer lab with a race to see who could get from a random Wikipedia page to "Jesus" in the fewest clicks, using only hyperlinks to hop around the site, like a frog jumping from lily pad to lily pad to cross a pond. She had a bizarre natural aptitude for deciphering cryptic bibliographic data. But the real secret to finding what you wanted fast was starting with the right kind of query. Learn to manipulate a few advanced search operators, and you could save yourself a lot of hours looking for a needle in a haystack.

She found a few of Kinnan's articles, and a few of Lockley's, distributed across a handful of medical and scientific journals. She skimmed the abstracts, but even those were alienating—a sort of biochemical inside baseball. Not her branch of science, but she picked up enough recurring keywords to run a new search better suited to a general audience. The first hit, to her surprise, came not from any of the more reputable encyclopedias to digitize their content but from an article in the *Belltower Times* five years ago. She frowned, unsure what any of her search terms had to do with "Two South Campus Dormitories Closed for Structural Damage." Only at the very bottom of the article did she find what she'd been looking for: *C. burranicum.* Several students had been quoted on the unpleasant enervating symptoms of exposure and the inconvenience of their forced evacuation, but one had other concerns: "'*C. burranicum* is an endemic species—it doesn't grow anywhere else,' according to sophomore biology major Wes Tucker, who was forced to leave his room on the fourth floor of Coblin Hall. 'Killing it would be like, mycological genocide.'"

A link in the article footer produced a list of other articles about campus closures due to fungal infestations. Tamar didn't know whether to be surprised when an article from a few months later listed the Calhoun Center as one of the buildings afflicted. This one had a picture. She woke up her phone and zoomed in on the photo of the mural from Edie, comparing it to the *Belltower*'s stock photo, which showed a crumbly whitish substance emerging from a fissure in a stone wall. It looked a little bit like rotting cauliflower, and a lot like the vegetal growth sprouting from the cracks in the Anchorite mural.

Tamar sat back in her chair. Tapped her fingers on the arms for a moment. There was some sort of connection—she just couldn't see it yet. Rats. Fungus. Pharmacology. Animal testing seemed the obvious answer, but why inter them in a churchyard in the middle of the night? Kinnan was evidently burying evidence, but of what? She looked at the clock. She wasn't going to find any answers sitting around the guest services desk. Nobody else was on duty, but nobody was due to check in either. She glanced up at the camera that monitored the lobby and reception. She was only allotted one twenty-minute break, and the Health Sciences Library was a ten-minute walk away. Not enough time to get there and back with anything worthwhile, even if she ran. She tapped her fingernails on the arms of the chair again. Thinking. Wondering what she had to lose besides a dead-end job. Her bra strap slipped off her shoulder, fell out of the sleeve of her gooseshit-green hospitality polo. She let it hang there, not in a sexy way but in an I've-had-this-bra-longer-than-I've-had-this-job sort of way. At least, it hadn't felt sexy until about an hour ago, when Hannah leaned across the console of the darkened car to slide it back up over the curve of her shoulder. Sometimes she dropped her off or picked her up, and that was all. But not always.

Her phone buzzed on the desk. Message from Edie: *WELL???*

Tamar chewed her lip. Tapped back, *Not sure yet.* She pulled up the same series of *Times* articles on her mobile browser, sent the link to the group. *Tuck, what else do you know about burranicum?*

Ellipses tiptoed across the screen. *Why?*

She sent a link to Kinnan's department page. *Because Kinnan knows something we don't.* And she wanted to know what. She checked the clock again, curiosity stirring in her blood.

Fuck it. They could sack her, for all she cared, because solving the mystery of several dozen dead rats was, suddenly, all she cared about. She put the plastic sign that said BACK IN 20 MINUTES on the desk and reached for her coat.

Outside, the cold wrapped tight around her like a winding sheet. She walked quickly, turning her collar up against a breeze that brushed its icy fingers across her cheek. But the chill was invigorating. Feeling deliciously reckless, she shook a fresh cigarette out of the pack in her pocket and lit up. Who gave a shit if she was within a hundred feet of half a dozen university buildings? Let the bumbling campus cops come and clap her in irons. The nicotine buzzed in her brain, made her blink her eyes open wider.

She pitched the butt into a trash can at the library's back entrance and swiped her key card to open the door. If anybody wanted to know why she was there after hours, she'd say she forgot something—her glasses, her phone charger, her professional ethics. Whatever. She flipped the lights on behind the circulation desk, booted up the computer, and watched all the paywalls come tumbling down. From inside the Health Sciences Library, she could access any major scientific publication and some unpublished material, too. Searching all the databases for "*C. burranicum*" turned up a few regional wildlife guides and a couple of chapters in larger volumes on mycology, phycology, and pharmacology.

She scanned the abstracts for anything that looked relevant and ran a couple of promising pages off the nearest printer. Then she added the word "rat," just to see what happened. The results shrank to one: a master's thesis from Rutgers penned by none other than Tom Kinnan. "Therapeutic Potentialities of Lichenicolous Fungi: *C. burranicum* and the Central Nervous System."

She downloaded a PDF from ProQuest and searched within the document for any "rats" lurking in the text. The first of several dozen results highlighted itself in the last line of the abstract: "Preliminary tests on male Long-Evans rats indicated no adverse side effects."

"Bingo." She hit print, closed out of the external databases, and logged into the library's loan system. Kinnan's account activity was fairly constant; he had almost two hundred books checked out and enough chapter requests to clog up the interlibrary pipeline for weeks. She hit print again, hit the lights, and snatched his thesis and his circulation history out of the tray on her way out the door.

Got some answers, lots more questions, she texted the group. *Might need an expert.*

Theo was the first to reply. *I've got one, but I might have gotten him too drunk to do much talking.*

Hannah was unusually quick to respond. *Could be you're just asking too nicely.*

Tamar shivered, but not from the cold.

2:20 AM
Hannah

Hannah drove a battered black Toyota that had been pulled apart and put back together so many times it constituted a philosophical conundrum. Was it still the same car she'd bought for a song ten years ago? For the last decade it had been her only constant companion. Friends and lovers came and went, but the Toyota was forever. When it first broke down, she signed up for auto shop and had it towed to the campus garage. That was the last class she enrolled in. Instead she joined an automotive technician training program and every rideshare app accepting drivers. Five years later she made a living under the hood and behind the wheel and never went back for a "real" degree. What for? The Toyota and a toolbox were all she needed to get by, and most "real" jobs that required "real" degrees didn't jibe with her circadian rhythm anyway. She was rarely out and about during daylight hours, adapted to a nocturnal existence of necessity.

Sleep had eluded her since girlhood. She spent countless black hours twisting in the grip of night terrors, screaming and shrinking from some invisible menace until she was un-ceremoniously submerged in cold water. By the time she was ten, her parents had given up on the sleep training touted by every child psychologist and abandoned her to the su-pervision of late-night TV. By the time she was twenty, she had given up on every sleep aid that promised to alleviate her insomnia. By the time she was thirty, she had given up trying, tired of being tired, tired of telling people she was tired, tired of being bombarded with imbecilic advice about how to be less tired. *Have you tried a warm bath? Warm milk? Herbal tea? Reading before bed always works for me!*

No, shit-for-brains, she wanted to say—and sometimes did, *I've only been trying to sleep since the day I was born, and googling home remedies never occurred to me.* Normies talked about melatonin like it was fucking propofol. Hannah had tried every sedative and depressant that was legal and quite a few that weren't. Nothing worked. She learned to live in the permanent twilight of sleep-deprivation psychosis. Life, if you could call it that, was a never-ending out-of-body experience.

The bump of the subwoofer anchored her in the driver's seat. She rolled to a stop under a glaring red light at the intersection of Foxglove and Azalea. Watched a clutch of coeds stumble across the street in skirts too short for the temperature, heels too high to walk in after the too many drinks they'd had. Unlike them, Hannah had adapted to the liquid elasticity of the after-midnight hours. Oncoming headlights bent at impossible angles; neon refracted off windows and windshields. Every shadow stretched and warped, like reflections in a fun house mirror. Laughter, music, the whole human imbroglio half smothered by the weight of darkness. She liked the world better that way.

The light changed and she drummed her fingers on the wheel as she lifted her foot off the brake. All digits accounted for, which meant she was, technically, awake. Her fingers had an unsettling tendency to vanish or multiply, to sprout scales or talons, on the rare occasions she slipped out of her body without realizing. Most people never traversed the numinous no-man's-land between sleep and waking, where the laws of the physical universe went to pieces. Hannah could have been a tour guide, there or on the terrestrial plane. Driving around all day and all night for years on end meant that she knew every blind alley and dark corner her zip code had to offer. Lyft and Uber tried to tell her where and how to drive; she always got there faster going her own way. But the bars were closed now, and she'd made her last pickup of the night—except one.

Her phone lit up in the cupholder. She'd silenced it hours ago, the incessant buzz of the group text itching under her skin. A couple of riders had slurred their words in the backseat as they asked each other, "Izzat you or me?" She glanced at the screen, thumbed through the most recent flurry of messages between Edie, Tuck, and Tamar with one hand on the wheel. Screenshots of news clippings, academic journals, Kinnan's library account. They had their methodology, but—as was the case with the GPS—Hannah could get there faster, unburdened by anybody else's rules. She cracked the window and lit a cigarette from the pack of Camels shoved in the busted cassette tray. She smoked wherever she wanted, didn't need the churchyard charade, but kept going back, for some reason. She'd stopped asking herself why, not much liking any of the plausible answers.

Occam's razor.

A new message from Theo interrupted the back-and-forth between Edie, Tuck, and Tamar. *Hannah, what's your ETA?*

Two minutes, she wrote back. *Walk him out.*

How many times had she been summoned to the Rocker Box to give some shit-faced barfly a safe lift home? Too many to count.

She swerved across oncoming traffic, made a reckless U-turn, and lurched to a stop with her front tire kissing the curb. The Toyota hummed impatiently; it never idled for long. The sidewalk outside the bar was empty—too late and too cold for anybody to linger. She leaned on the console with one elbow, flicked her ash out the window. Scrolled through her playlists for a little background music to suit the mood. Concrete Blonde, of course. It was a bloodletting kind of an evening.

The door to the bar swung open. Hannah dropped her phone, lowered the passenger window. Theo helped Kinnan to the car, saying, "See, Uber's already here. You'll be home before you know it." Kinnan muttered something indistinct as Theo opened the back door, pushing his head down so he didn't hit the window frame. He'd have wicked déjà vu when the time for his perp walk came. Hannah had no doubts he was up to his eyeballs in something illegal. Took one to know one, perhaps. Then again, she knew more about poor Tom than any of the rest of them—even Tamar. Not that anyone needed to know that. Not yet, anyway. Not until she knew more.

"Thanks," Theo said to Hannah, slamming the door once Kinnan's arms and legs were accounted for.

"All in a night's work," she said snidely. Kinnan lolled against his seat, too drunk to notice anything odd about their interaction.

A wan little smile from Theo. "Drive safe."

Hannah gave him the finger and peeled away. She took the first turn sharply, watching in the rearview mirror as Kinnan swayed one way, then the other. He settled against the seat again when she straightened the wheel, head thrown back, eyes closed. She turned the music down to a murmur. Oncoming headlights bloomed through the windshield, then faded away. She took another left turn. Then a right. Then another left. Watching Kinnan's head wobble on his neck like it wasn't securely attached. After two more turns, he snuffled, snorted, and started to snore. Hannah smirked at her reflection. Candy from a baby.

She turned onto a narrow, unmarked road, far enough now from the lights of downtown that the night settled heavily over the car. No more oncoming headlights—just the elusive quicksilver of the waning moon. Hannah's phone blinked on and off in the cupholder as the rest of the Anchorites jabbered at one another, but she ignored it. Their Scooby-Doo sleuthing might turn up some answers eventually, but why wait? Let the kids keep meddling. The adults had some talking to do.

Bothell Forest occupied several hundred acres of land on the north side of town. According to the signs, the trails closed at sundown, but there were no fences, no gates, no enforcement. She took the first fork away from the overlook, where there were always one or two other cars hosting little indiscretions of their own—drug deals and prostitution and garden-variety infidelity. Hannah, on the other hand, was prepared to do something rather more drastic if Kinnan didn't cooperate, and she didn't want to be interrupted.

She parked the car on a gravelly shoulder under a stand of shortleaf pines. Left the engine running and left her phone in the cupholder. When she climbed out of the car, her skin seemed to tighten in defense against the cold. She took her time taking the last couple of drags on her cigarette and ground the butt beneath her heel. The straight black trunks of the trees surrounded the car, a blue wash of mist creeping over the roots. The Toyota sunk to the bumpers in the brume. Hannah swung her feet as she walked around the car, like a child kicking through the surf. Kinnan was still sound asleep, slumped against the window. In for a rude awakening, but not just yet.

She eased the back door open, trusting the noble Toyota not to give her away. She didn't need to open it far. She'd never eaten or weighed enough—one warmongering brother still called her Olive Oyl. Maybe it suited her. She'd always been slippery. Kinnan didn't hear or feel her slide onto the seat beside him. One ear smashed against the window, his breath a sour cloud of white on the glass. Thankfully, Theo had made no effort to wrestle him into his gloves. His phone was easy to find, poking up out of his coat pocket like he'd just stashed it there for a moment.

Text from Heather: *Tom, what the fuck is going on?*

My, my. A bit informal for a faculty advisor. But Heather—dear Heather—could wait.

Hannah pressed Kinnan's thumb to his phone's fingerprint scanner, gently and just long enough for it to unlock. He shifted, mumbled. She opened the settings menu and checked the screen-lock timer. Fifteen minutes. She didn't think she'd need that long, but tucked the phone in her outer pocket, where she could tap it awake if she needed to. Still, Kinnan snored. He looked terrible, she was pleased to see. More gray in his hair than the last time she saw him, going jowly around the chin and trying to hide it behind the beard. His shirt was missing a button, but it had acquired a few unmistakable mustard stains. Fastidious Mr. Kinnan reduced to a slob. None of that offended her, particularly. It was the depth, the weight, the ostentatious *ease* of his sleep. Over the river and through the woods, and he was out cold. She'd stolen his whole life right out of his pocket and he didn't even know.

She listened to his breathing. Long and slow. Wallowing like a pig in his excess of rest.

A flash of rage consumed her so suddenly a cold sweat broke out on her chest. The soft, weird glow of her phone pulsed through the car. The trees gathered in close like so many curious cryptids. Hannah, home again among the monsters. She grabbed the seat belt by the latch plate, looped it once around Kinnan's neck, and yanked it tight. He choked himself awake, eyes popping out of his head like a cartoon character.

"You forgot to fasten your seat belt," she said, and jerked it tighter when he started to squirm. He wheezed thinly through his nose, the fight already going out of him. Worried she'd break his neck before she strangled him? Who knew. She'd never done this before and neither had he, probably. "Got a couple of questions for you, Tom," she told him, with a little tug she hoped he found persuasive. "Loosen your tongue and I'll loosen the belt, understand?"

He gave her a whimper, which she took for a yes.

"We'll start with something easy: Remember me?"

He blinked, eyes streaming into his beard. "*No*," he managed to say.

"That's annoying, I make a point not to be the sort of girl you forget in a hurry."

"*No*," he gurgled again. That incandescent anger peeled her nerves apart like split ends. She could smell her own sweat, and his.

"I'm one of your lab rats, Tom. I'm the ghost of lab rats past." He went still, stopped struggling. Hannah blew a kiss in his ear. "Honey, do you remember me now?"

What a charming name they gave it. Project Honeydew. That must have been Heather's idea. She had the same cold, sticky sweetness. She insisted everyone call her Heather, not Dr. Lockley. Even slippery little rats like Hannah.

Kinnan gave another doglike whine, which she decided, again, to take as a yes.

"Good. What about the other rats, the ones you buried in the churchyard? You must not be a smoker or you'd know better." She loosened the seat belt, ever so slightly. "Speak up! Don't be shy."

"We always—euthanize—lab animals."

"But you don't usually dig them a grave. Why the ceremony?" He hesitated just a moment too long. She squeezed the seat belt tighter. Fighting the urge to tighten it further, half hoping he'd give her a reason. "Spit it out!"

"Contaminated!"

"Try again." She gave him a sharp yank this time. "That's what the incinerators are for."

"Not—toxic—not—infectious—"

"I'll take 'Mycological' for one thousand, Tom." It was starting to make sense to her now. Project Honeydew was a way to explore the therapeutic potential of one lichenicolous fungus. "Tell me about *burranicum*." She'd gleaned enough from even a cursory glance at Tamar's findings. *Burranicum* alkaloids acted on the central nervous system to produce a euphoric, soporific effect. Honeydew recruited patients with a history of chronic, drug-resistant insomnia and paid them each a paltry sum for their participation. Hannah didn't care about the money, and she had nothing to lose but more sleep. She'd signed the consent forms without even reading them.

"—can't breathe—"

She relaxed her grip, barely. "I know what it was supposed to do," she said. Because Heather had explained it in comprehensive, *loving* detail. She believed in this drug. It could cure people like Hannah, unlock the door to sweet serenity. She administered most doses herself, tilting Hannah back in her chair, lifting her eyelid with one gloved finger. Lurking beneath the antiseptic smell of latex, a whisper of perfume clung to the soft white skin inside her wrist. Bitter orange, vanilla, and vetiver. No less intoxicating than the pipette of greenish serum. Three drops in each eye, and the world dissolved into kaleidoscopic dreams. When she woke, Heather was always there, like she'd never left, bending over her with a tissue. *Hold still,* she'd say, with such a tender smile. *You've got sleep in your eyes.* Hannah pushed the memory aside. She couldn't let her grip slacken too much. "I'm really more interested in what it *wasn't* supposed to do."

"You—slept," Kinnan choked. Oddly insistent about that. Or indignant, maybe. "It—*worked.*" And so it had, until they closed the program without warning or explanation. "It was—*helping* people—like you."

People like her. He could fall asleep in less than five minutes in a moving car with a stranger behind the wheel. What the hell did he know about people like her?

"Until it didn't," she said, cinching the belt around his thick neck. He used to have a chin. And she used to count down the days until her appointments with Lockley, her next dose of Honeydew. Only to return to counting sleepless hours when they cut her off, cold turkey. "The study was supposed to be three months. Why shut it down?"

"Too many—long-term—side effects."

"Like what?" They'd stopped the study weeks ago. She had blamed the headaches, the palpitations, the swimming vision, on withdrawal from the drug. She'd always been irritable—chronic insomnia did that to a person—but rarely angry. Anger took energy. Anger took effort. She couldn't afford to expend excess energy or effort on anything, but lately she couldn't help herself. Lately she'd been angry. "Is that what happened to the rats?" When Kinnan hesitated, she tightened the belt again.

"No! Different dose—new formula—"

She jerked the belt. "What happened to the rats, Tom?"

He gurgled. Grunted. Talked faster. "—mycotoxins— attacked—the neocortex—but—"

"Plain English, Tom. Some of us never finished college."

"—normative—social behavior—broke down—"

"Broke down how?"

"—aggression—hostility—cannibalism—"

Hannah ran her tongue across her teeth. Her mouth tasted like metal. "How long did it take?" she asked. The word *hostility* echoing between her ears. "For the good rats to go bad." Kinnan didn't answer, but she hadn't changed her grip. He was beginning to sober up. She twisted the belt, heard him gag. Tamped down another powerful urge to keep twisting. "How long, Tom."

"Ages," he gasped. "Didn't know—such a long— incubation." His voice was hoarse but high. Almost keening. "Thought—it was—safe."

"I don't care what you thought," Hannah told him. "I care how long I have before I'm just another Hostile Incident." It didn't take a genius to make the leap, with a few of the blanks filled in. Several weary, mild-mannered people going suddenly berserk. She swallowed. Her heart throbbed in her throat. She didn't know how much more she could squeeze out of him, and her fifteen minutes were running down. "What are the warning signs? Before it escalates to full-blown brain damage."

"I told you," he gasped. "Hostility—aggress—"

"Before that. Other symptoms, other signs it's progressing."

"—mycelial—growth—" He was working hard to say so many long words with so little air. "—temporary—blindness—"

"Is there any way to stop it, slow it down?"

"Don't know—nothing—so far."

Then she had no further use for him. She opened the door, let go of the seat belt, and shoved him out of the car. Before he even hit the ground, she'd slammed the other door behind her and jumped back into the driver's seat. She revved the engine and reversed off the shoulder, back onto the lonely, winding road. Kinnan scrambled to his feet and hollered after her, but she wasn't going back. "Don't wait up," she said, and glanced at his phone, still unlocked, still faintly aglow. His home screen showed the date and time and temperature. The night was half over, and the cold wasn't cold enough to kill him. Probably. She watched his reflection shrink in the rearview mirror until the dim crimson taillights left him behind and darkness swallowed him whole.

Don't worry, she texted back to Heather. *Everything's under control.*

3:30 AM

Edie

Edie persuaded Tuck to go along to the newspaper office on the grounds that he should disinfect the bites and scratches on his hands and there was a first aid kit in the break room—no health insurance required. Theo was still stuck in the Box and would be the rest of the night, on account of an "arduous apology" he had to make before closing alone. No word from Hannah since she'd picked up Kinnan. Yes, she was driving, but that had never stopped her from texting before. Everyone was acting out of character. Tamar had simply abandoned the reception desk and seemed unconcerned about the consequences. She came straight from the library, and Edie put her to work with Tuck, hoping they could combine their weird superpowers to make some sense of Kinnan's research. If Tamar could unpick the jargon, maybe Tuck could demystify the science. Edie erased the whiteboard and squeaked across it with a red dry-erase marker. FACTS? it asked. *Salva veritate.* So far, the list was short.

Edie cracked her third can of Diet Coke. Forget the cigarettes, maybe that was what was giving her cancer—if it was cancer, which it probably wasn't, statistically speaking. FACTS! She sighed, slugged the Coke anyway. FACT: Diet Coke had more caffeine than regular, but still much less than coffee. FACT: That did not make it any better for you. FACT: Edie did not care. If she could make the story hang together, it could turn everything else around. If she had a good story, they might be in the running for another Pacemaker. If they were in the running for another Pacemaker, her worth as editor-in-chief wouldn't be so much in question. If her worth as editor-in-chief wasn't so much in question, her self-worth probably wouldn't be either. If her self-worth was a little less shaky, she might be a little less freaked out about The Lump that was probably nothing. Probably. In any case, she didn't care what combination of carcinogens it took—she was going to get the story straight if it was the last thing she did. FACT.

She had dumped a pile of snacks on the conference table along with the first aid kit. Tamar had chosen a Clif bar and bottled water and looked right at home there with her glasses on and her hair pinned on top of her head with an artfully twisted pencil. Tuck, on the other hand, had lived in the damp and the dark long enough that he squinted and cowered like a cave-dwelling salamander underneath the stark fluorescent lights. Edie had slathered the scratches and bites with peroxide and topical anesthetic, but his hands were still shaking. He'd eaten two bags of peanut M&M's one at a time and tore into a third automatically.

"I don't get it." Tamar had Kinnan's master's thesis fanned in front of her, the most relevant passages outlined in green highlighter. They'd been at it about an hour, and Edie had about four more before she would have to go chase down comments if she wanted the story online in the afternoon and on doorsteps the next day. "What exactly is he trying to prove? According to him and according to you, the sedative-hypnotic properties of C. *burranicum* have been a known quantity since before the colonists."

Tuck shook his head. "A known quantity is exactly what it isn't," he crunched, mouth full of candy. "It's been used in folk medicine for centuries, but that's the thing about folk medicine—it's totally unregulated. So, yeah, if it's the Civil War you might crush it to a powder and chug it with some small beer before the doctor comes to saw your legs off, but not an exact science, no."

"So that's what Kinnan's doing, then," Tamar suggested. "Trying to turn it into an exact science."

"Right. It's a thing in pharmacology, mining traditional medicine for kernels of truth that can be bottled and labeled and sold to the Sacklers for a cool billion dollars. Then sold to all of us with a name like Xanotrax or Ziphoquil or whatever."

"Like biomedical cultural appropriation."

"Right."

"Right," Edie said, "but where do the rats come in?"

"I don't know about *these* rats"—Tamar looked uneasily toward the fridge, where they were doing their best to cryogenically preserve the late Tuck Jr., on the off chance he proved useful—"but six years ago, when he was still at Rutgers, he was testing different concentrations to try to determine a therapeutic dose. And he had quite a lot of trouble, mostly because individual tolerance is wildly variable."

"The bioavailability of the fungal metabolites trips him up, too," Tuck pointed out.

"Is that why *burranicum* never caught on?" Edie asked. "There are just much better anesthetics out there."

"He's not interested in anesthesia," Tuck said. "Look at this table—he's interested in circadian rhythm regulation. Sleep-wake cycles."

"But he's also interested in hormones—here, that's this appendix—which seems to be why he's using this strain of lab rat in particular," Tamar explained.

"What?" Edie looked blankly from her to Tuck. She was majoring in journalism for a reason.

"Long-Evans rats are bred by crossing lab rats with wild rats, which makes them—so far as I understand it—closer to wild animals in their behavior, and especially their social behavior."

"Something about higher levels of certain hormones and stronger responses to external stressors," Tuck said.

"Such as?" Edie asked. They were losing her. Or maybe she was losing them. She couldn't tell. She'd been working long hours of late but rarely the whole night, sundown to sunup, even if that meant napping with her head down on her desk. So far removed from the Anchorite, the adrenaline had worn off, and the Diet Coke, despite its higher caffeine quotient, wasn't doing much to mitigate the fatigue.

"Sleep deprivation, for one." Tuck started to rub his eyes with his scratched hands, then thought better of it—skin already pink and swollen. Who knew what kind of chemical hocus-pocus he might be smearing across his corneas? "He concludes that with just the right concentration of *burranicum* administered just the right way, it could be an effective, nonaddictive alternative to benzos and Z-drugs and not looking at your phone for half an hour before bed."

"But, naturally," Tamar added, flipping to the last page in the packet, "'Further research is needed.'"

"Which is why he hooks up with Dr. Lockley at the Calhoun Center." Edie had pulled Lockley's faculty profile up on her laptop and projected it onto the whiteboard. She was in her middle forties, judging by the year she finished her doctorate. She wore her hair long—voluminous brown curls that looked like they'd be a hazard in the laboratory—with a pair of oversize tortoiseshell glasses that only emphasized her allure. Lockley was, whatever her shortcomings, objectively beautiful. And objectively beautiful people could bend the rules in a way objectively average people could not. FACT.

And, in fact, Dr. Lockley had a reputation for pushing the envelope before she was even hired. Trawling through back issues of the *Times*, Edie had unearthed an article about Lockley's appointment. "Maverick Neurologist Joins Pendell School of Medicine." She'd highlighted one intriguing pull quote in particular: "Others expressed reservations about Lockley. A source from inside the Calhoun Center, who spoke with the *Times* on the condition of anonymity, warned that 'Lockley's methods are controversial for a reason—it's dangerous, out there on the bleeding edge of everything, and I wonder if it's worth risking the reputation of the university.'"

A little internet sleuthing had turned up a few more articles that fawned over Lockley's "groundbreaking" research and "unusual" methods. Details were few and far between, but Lockley herself had, in one interview, admitted to conducting off-the-clock "mesearch" into different forms of psychedelic therapy. "I'm still my own guinea pig, sometimes, sure. In science and medicine we like to pretend it's all very impersonal, but the truth is it's rare you find anyone with a purely academic interest in this stuff. You get interested because it's personal, and once you turn it into a profession, you have to pretend it isn't personal anymore. That never felt right to me. Who better to do the work than someone with a vested interest in the outcome?" She laughed off the interviewer's next question about administrative red tape. "Well, to be an innovator, you have to be a bit of an iconoclast, I suppose. Galileo died on house arrest for suggesting that the earth revolved around the sun, which went against the holy rule of Rome."

That seemed reasonable enough to Edie, but Tuck had a very different reaction. All his twitches and tics became more pronounced, his scattered nervous energy momentarily finding laser-like focus. "*That* is not good science," he said, throwing an M&M at Lockley's picture. "It's exactly that kind of science, actually, that gives alternative therapies a bad name. They're so keen to be on the bleeding fucking edge they end up setting everyone else back decades. People like Timothy Leary, who just can't wait to smuggle it all out of the lab." He fired another M&M across the room and hit his mark. It bounced off Lockley's forehead and rolled away under the fridge where the rat was slowly going stiff. But it was Tamar who sat up bolt upright, as if she'd been electrocuted.

"Wait!" she said, and Edie recognized that light in her eyes, which meant that two pieces of the puzzle had clicked together in her mind. "What if that's exactly what happened here?"

Tuck paused in the windup for his next pitch. "What's exactly what happened here?"

"Something escaping the lab," Tamar said, shuffling through the papers on the table at speed, shoving them out of her way as soon as she saw they weren't what she was looking for. Edie said nothing, loath to interrupt and risk derailing her train of thought. She crossed her fingers under the table. "I mean, why bury the rats? Why not just incinerate them? Lockley might like to think of herself as a maverick, but flouting that policy wouldn't prove anything. There must be another motive."

"Which brings us right back to where we started," Tuck said. "With a pile of dead rats in a graveyard and no idea why." He lobbed another M&M at the whiteboard. His aim left a lot to be desired, and Edie winced as it disappeared behind a filing cabinet. If she didn't want live rats coming to join their frozen comrade, someone would need to vacuum. She pushed it out of her mind; that was what freshmen were for.

"I don't know about *no* idea," Tamar said. "Because I've got a crazy one."

Which reminded Edie, still no word from Hannah. She chose not to dwell on that.

"Why not?" Tuck asked. "Everything else about this is crazy."

"Occam's razor," Edie told him. "Lay it on me."

"So, looking at Kinnan's library account, there's nothing out of the ordinary before about six weeks ago," Tamar said, riffling through the sheaf of pages she'd printed at Health Sciences circulation. "Everything he's checking out and turning in fits in with what we know he's working on. Sleep-wake and endocrine disorders, systems biology, alternative medicine, blah blah blah. Some stuff for classes he's teaching, some stuff that looks like it might be for Lockley."

Tuck frowned. "So, what happens six weeks ago?"

"Well, about six weeks ago, all the keywords change, and so does the volume of material. He's coming in every two days, not every two weeks, and what he's reading takes a very, um, *macabre* turn."

"Macabre how?" Edie asked, looking sideways at Tuck's swollen hands. Looking sideways at the minifridge. Not sure how much more macabre it could get.

"I mean, Tuck's the mycologist, but 'zombie fungi'? Seems pretty grim to me."

A twitch of a grin from Tuck. "They attack ants, mostly. Hijack their little ant brains to make them latch onto a plant where the fungus can propagate."

"But he's also looking into cortical lesions, seizures . . . something called rage syndrome." Tamar's eyes tracked rapidly back and forth across the pages for another moment or two before she looked up. "I'm not a doctor, but that sounds serious."

"You know what else it sounds like?" Edie said. Because she understood where Tamar was going, now. She was right—it *did* seem crazy—but Edie was willing to follow her there. *Salva veritate!* Truth, she had learned in her time at the paper, was almost always stranger than fiction. She opened a new tab, which automatically landed on the *Belltower Times* home page. She added "/hostile-incidents" to the end of the URL and scrolled through the series, reading her own headlines aloud. "'Stadium Custodian Attacks Ticketholders.' 'Brawl Breaks Out at Farmers' Market.'

'Road Rage on Library Drive.' 'Latest Hostile Incident Closes Rocker Box.'"

"Hold on," Tuck said. "You think Lockley and Kinnan were testing this shit on *people?*"

"Why not?" Edie asked. "It's not a controlled substance—it's growing all over the Anchorite. It was growing in the basement of your dorm. Didn't you say you can buy it at that weird new agey health store on Lupine?"

"Not at this kind of concentration," Tuck said, shaking his head. "Nobody's selling Serum of Psychoactive Parasitic Fungus out of Spiritual-Healings-R-Us. You have to go through all kinds of quality control before you graduate from rats to human subjects."

"Yeah," Edie said, "unless you're a maverick."

"That would explain why they buried the rats instead of incinerating them," Tamar said. "No paper trail, no raised eyebrows. The rats just decompose, and when they do, any traces of *burranicum* left return to the soil, where it's already growing. Nobody the wiser." She shrugged. "It's not a *great* plan, but Kinnan's a graduate student, not a criminal mastermind."

"That's the only theory we've come up with that would explain everything," Edie said.

"It's a hell of a theory," Tuck said, and tossed another M&M at the whiteboard. "But except for one dead rat, we don't have any actual *proof*."

Edie opened her mouth to answer but was interrupted by all three of their phones buzzing in unison. Message to them and to Theo, but not to the Anchorites group text. She didn't recognize the number. Someone had sent a screenshot of a text conversation. Then another, and then another. Then emails, lab reports, search histories started pouring in.

"What is this?" Tamar asked.

"*Who* is this?" Tuck said.

Edie couldn't scroll back to the top fast enough—new messages kept coming. "It looks like—"

"No, how could it—"

"Are these texts from Kinnan to Lockley?"

"That email sure is."

"Shit, this one has *photos*."

"Who the hell is sending these?"

"Wait!" Tamar grabbed Edie's phone out of her hand and scrolled through both text chains side by side. "What's the area code for New Hampshire?"

Edie typed the question into the search bar. "603," she said. "Why?"

Tamar looked up. "I think these are coming from Kinnan."

"No way." She snatched her phone back. A dozen more images had come through.

"Look here, where Theo sent that picture of his driver's license. See? New Hampshire. And this area code? 603."

"But why would he—"

Their phones buzzed again, at the exact same time. Text from the mysterious 603.

78

Have I got a scoop for you bitches

Unbelievably, Edie felt herself smiling. "That's not Kinnan," she said. "That's Hannah." It had to be. Never before had Edie been happy, so happy, to hear from her. She clapped her hands hard enough to make Tuck jump. "Now we're in business."

"*Now?*" Tuck said, looking stricken. "*Now* we're in business? It's four in the morning, Edie!"

"So no time to waste," she said, still scrolling madly through the screenshots sent by 603. "But if we divide and conquer, it'll go faster. I'll start drafting something—I've spent so much time on this Hostile Incident nonsense I can do that part with my eyes closed—if you two can find me anything incriminating that might tie Kinnan's rat rage back to the other Belligerents. Sound good?" She looked up again to find them staring back at her. Tamar with her eyebrows pinched together, Tuck scratching at the back of his neck with one swollen hand.

"Edie, it really doesn't," Tamar said. "I know you're excited to have a story, but . . ."

"But what?" She glanced from her to Tuck.

"They're not just . . . Belligerents or Hostile Incidents," he said. "They're people. Remember? That's kinda why there's a story in the first place."

Her face stung like he'd slapped her. Heart rattling in her ears. She was never lost for words; words spilled out of her without pause, flowed from her tongue and her fingers and her keyboard as fast and as fluidly as she breathed. But how many times had her internal word processor gotten the better of her better judgment? "I—" she blurted. "Sorry. I'm sorry. You're right. Sorry. I'm—I'll be back, I'm just going to take a break. I mean, you don't have to stay. Sorry." That seemed to be the only word she could say now, *sorry*.

She backed out of the conference room and shut herself in her office. She left the overhead lights off. Her stomach gurgled unpleasantly. Too much soda. She closed her eyes, but they wouldn't stay still, rolling and vibrating behind their lids the way they did when she'd been staring at a screen for too long. She bent her knees and sank down on the floor between the file cabinet and a recycling bin full of empties. Coke cans and coffee cups and crumpled sheets of yellow paper torn off her legal pad. She knew without looking. Creature of habit.

Her eyes opened reluctantly. How long since she'd closed them for longer than it took to blink? She didn't want to know. What must it feel like, she wondered, for the first time and much too late, to be so desperate for rest that you'd let a doctor like Lockley drop her experimental poison in your eyes? She pulled the bottom drawer of the filing cabinet open. The Hostile Incidents folder was close to the front. She took it out and flipped through it again, slowly this time, lingering over each column, each page of interview notes.

Curtis Brandle had worked at the stadium as a custodian for twelve years. He had no criminal record and no family history of mental illness. Coworkers described him as cheerful. He listened to the Pointer Sisters while he mopped. His daughter was a sophomore.

Sandra Lanyon was a nanny before she tried to strangle a man ahead of her in line at the orchard stand. Her clients loved her like a daughter and trusted her enough to take her on family vacations. She was studying to be a speech pathologist and engaged to be married to her high school sweetheart in March.

Alma Pereira was the best medical interpreter the ER had ever had. She spoke five languages and had lived in more countries than most people could name. She played pop culture podcasts on the drive to work until a cyclist cut her off in traffic and she tried to run him over.

Zack Taft had one semester left in his MBA, which he planned to take back to Maine to modernize his family's fishery business. He was a strictly social drinker and a not-so-strict pescatarian. His brother was killed by a brain tumor when he was fifteen.

Edie felt, after the mold and the rats and the cigs and the soda, queasy for the first time all night. The *Times* had brainwashed her. A little zombie fungus of her own that scrambled her priorities beyond recognition. Tuck was right; she'd lost sight of the whole point of breaking a story like this, which was not the paper or the Pacemaker or The Lump under her arm that was probably just a lump. The people were the point.

Edie glanced sideways through the frosted glass and was surprised—but not much—to see Tuck and Tamar, still there, heads still bent over the conference table. She ran her fingers through the roots of her hair. Rubbed her eyes. "Shit," she said softly. She owed it to them, to Curtis and Sandra and Alma and Zack, to finish what she'd started and do it right, *salva veritate!* With truth intact.

FACT.

3:50 AM
Theo

Theo had turned off the OPEN sign, turned off the algorithmic mix of recent hits they played in the Box during business hours, and put on *Private Dancer* instead. Tina was his only solace when he was feeling sentimental and sorry for himself. He picked at a basket of cold hush puppies while he wiped down the tables and the bar, stacked glasses and chairs, changed a couple of kegs, took the empties out. It could have waited until morning, but sleep seemed impossibly distant. Since he'd been breaking his own rules lately, he broke another and lit a cigarette inside. When he'd sucked it down to the filter, he lit another. And another. And another. He smoked half the pack without pause, his eyes burning and his throat raw. He soft-shoed across the floor with the Swiffer, crooning hoarsely along to "Rock 'n'

Roll Widow." He spun the mop and dipped it like Ginger Rogers, looked up just in time to see Hannah standing in the doorway.

She cocked her head. He dropped the mop.

"Thought I might pop in for a nightcap, but if you're entertaining . . ."

"If I pour you a drink, will you shut up?"

"Can't drink and talk at the same time."

"Then belly up."

She perched on a stool and took a couple of hush puppies while he set a glass and a bottle of barrel proof rye on the bar. She probably didn't even need a glass. Hannah always drank like she was trying to die. She helped herself to one of his Marlboros and lit up, blew smoke out of the side of her mouth and said, in her best Scarlett O'Hara, "Surely you're too much a gentleman to make a lady drink alone."

Since he'd already broken his rule about sleeping with coworkers and his rule about smoking inside, why not get high on his own supply? Bad habits came in threes. He filled a second glass and raised it. "To what?" he asked.

"To whatever," she said, and cracked her glass against his. They drank, wiped their mouths, set their glasses down. Hannah filled them this time.

"Where's Kinnan?" he asked. Not at all certain he wanted to know.

"Dropped him off."

"A cliff?"

"You flatter me." She gave him a wicked little grin,

running one fingertip around the rim of her glass. He'd rarely seen her so playful, and it was always dangerous when Hannah showed her teeth. "I left him on the north side of town."

"Was he still in one piece?" He didn't quite understand it—the venom in her voice, her more-than-usual loathing of Tom Kinnan. Most people were beneath her notice, never mind her disdain.

"I can't speak for his psychic integrity."

"I hope you at least got something good out of him."

"I guess you haven't checked your phone."

He reached for the glass again. "My phone's gotten me in enough trouble for one night."

"I'm sure you'll be able to read all about it in the morning."

"Edie's unrelenting, isn't she."

"Why do you think I'm not at the newspaper office with the rest of them?"

"Because your only people skills are seduction and sadism."

She licked her lips. "What's the difference?"

"I don't know," he admitted. "I was accused of 'criminal carelessness' by the last woman to sit where you're sitting."

"Chelsea?"

"Who else?" He poured two more drinks, splashing whiskey all over the bar he'd just wiped down. Criminally careless. Might as well earn it.

"I knew I liked her," Hannah said.

He swirled the whiskey around. "So did I." Why lie? Hannah would mock him no matter what he said.

Predictably, she rolled her eyes. "Chin up, it's not like she's died."

"Think I might be dead to her, though."

"Give her time," she said, after another long slug of rye. "Be your usual charming self and maybe she'll change her mind. Or maybe don't be your usual charming self. How did you screw this up, anyway?"

"I honestly don't know. I can't figure out what she wants from me, or I'd do it. No matter what I say, it seems to be wrong."

"You're allowed to ask."

He stared across the bar at her. "Ask what?"

"What she wants." She stubbed out her cigarette. "Straight men are so stupid. Women aren't complicated. If you don't know how to get to where you want to be with her, just fucking ask for directions." She threw back the last of her drink. "I think that's enough talk therapy. You're welcome, I'll send you a bill."

"Oh, so you'll be paying for those drinks, then," he said.

"Put it on my tab for when hell freezes over."

"Remind me why I'm taking relationship advice from you?"

"I agree, it's embarrassing. Pull yourself together, Pavlopoulos." She smacked him on the shoulder. Bizarrely, he did feel better. Hannah had a way of making everything

86

serious seem absolutely absurd. He was about to pour a fourth round when his phone started to rattle on the back-bar. He turned it over, frowned at the name on the screen.

"I should take this," he said. "Hey, Hannah—" But she was already off her stool and halfway out the door, disappearing into the night without a backward glance. So it always went with her. He wedged his phone under one ear. "Jordan, hi." She was one of a regular group of hospital residents who'd been drinking in the Box on Tuesday, and stuck around to do minor first aid until the ambulance left. She'd promised to call back with news about their Belligerent.

"Listen, I don't have a lot of time," she said. "But I thought you should know, Zack Taft?"

He turned the music off, poured the last mouthful of whiskey down the sink. Reminding himself he had rules for a reason. "What about him?"

"He's dead."

Theo dropped the glass in the basin, where it broke with a dull, flat crack. "What?"

"It happened just now." He heard the quaver in her voice.

"How?"

"He had another one of his violent spells, then started convulsing. Grand mal seizure. Cardiac arrest. Never regained consciousness."

"Jesus. Jordan, I'm so sorry."

"I've never seen anything like it," she said, with a small

strangled gasp. Then calmed herself, spoke more steadily. "And I hope I never see anything like it again. He—" She stopped. "Sorry. Gotta go."

"No no no, *wait*—" But she was gone. Like Chelsea, like Hannah, like Kinnan and Zack Taft and everyone else who stopped by the Box. Nobody but Theo ever lingered for long. He fished the broken glass out of the sink, pitched it into the trash. Turned Tina back on.

6:30 AM

Tamar

Tamar hadn't slept all night. She'd smoked a whole pack and eaten nothing that hadn't come from a vending machine for twelve hours. What little makeup she still wore was smeared around her eyes and caked in the creases on her forehead, the laugh lines that bracketed her lips. Her hair was—she shuddered to even think the phrase—a rat's nest. Her clothes could be fresher, but her breath was much worse. She slurped at the sour black coffee she'd bought from the first place she passed with an OPEN sign on her walk from the *Belltower Times* to the Calhoun Center. Lockley held office hours from seven to eight, a clever scheduling maneuver that ensured nobody would actually come, leaving her free to check her email and play God for a while before teaching an early bio class on "The Physician's Garden:

Botany and Human Cell Biology." The course description promised guest lectures from pharmaceutical professionals and visits to the botanical gardens and was so cheerfully innocent it might have been penned by Beatrix Potter.

Tamar checked her watch. Not long now.

She had opened a map of the building on her phone and guessed that Lockley was most likely to come through the doors on the south side of the building, which opened into the stairwell closest to her office on the third floor. If she didn't see Lockley in the next ten minutes, she planned to go up and knock. Bedraggled as she was, she might pass for a student in the grip of a perilous hangover, if Lockley's eyesight was as bad as her Coke-bottle glasses implied.

Tamar almost didn't recognize her without them. Evidently, they were for reading or merely a prop to make her look more . . . professorial? Approachable? Bohemian? More like a lovable eccentric and less like a mad scientist, perhaps. Tamar pitched her cigarette into a nearby hedge as Lockley's heels clop-clopped, like horseshoes, up the walkway. She had a sheaf of papers in her arms and a deceptively expensive handbag slung over one shoulder. She walked right past Tamar without looking at her, shucking her gloves off and rooting around in her coat pockets for her key card to swipe herself into the building.

"Excuse me, Dr. Lockley?"

Lockley turned, looked down the steps at Tamar with a pinched sort of smile. "Yes, can I help you?"

"I hope so," Tamar said. "I'm reporting on a piece for the *Belltower Times*—"

"If you send me an email, I'm sure we can set something up," Lockley said. She had a low, melodious voice but spoke very quickly—the effect was incongruous, disorienting. How did her students take notes? But that was part of her magnetism, Tamar supposed—keep them leaning in and hanging on every word until they were converted. Poor Tom Kinnan didn't stand a chance.

"It won't take a minute—we're hoping to go to press this afternoon."

"I'm sorry, but I simply don't have a minute this morning—one of my TAs has gone AWOL with half my students' midterms."

"Do you mean Tom Kinnan?"

Lockley's hands went still, bag heavy in the crook of her elbow. "Do you know where he is?"

"Afraid not," Tamar admitted. Hannah had finally texted back, but she had already decided not to ask. "And since we really would like a comment from someone involved with Project Honeydew, we thought we'd come to you."

The effect of the phrase was worth the sleepless night, worth the half hour Tamar had been standing around the stairwell in the cold. Lockley's eyes widened, then narrowed; her mouth opened, then closed. Tamar couldn't help thinking how much more amusing it would have been with her enormous glasses on, but no matter. In an instant she'd smoothed her ruffled exterior, expression as cool and placid as a pond frozen over in winter. "I'm sorry," she said, "I don't know what you're talking about."

"Let me refresh your memory, then," Tamar said pleasantly. She handed over a manila folder containing the most incriminating emails, texts, and screenshots sent from Kinnan's phone. Lockley leafed through it, slowly at first and then faster, the color draining from her face until the loose papers slipped from her fingers and scattered themselves across the sidewalk. She made a grab for the nearest page and crumpled it in her fist, but the rest escaped and went whirling away down the street. Tamar watched them turn somersaults in the breeze, unbothered. They could always print more.

"Where exactly did you get all this . . ." Lockley seemed at a loss for words, so Tamar provided one for her.

"Evidence? I realize research ethics aren't your strong suit, but you know journalists aren't obliged to divulge their sources." She smiled. She wasn't a journalist, but she was warming to the role. She'd volunteered to go so Edie could post her article as soon as they had what they wanted from Lockley. Waiting around with nothing to do but smoke had gotten her thinking. Maybe it wasn't such a long leap from library science to investigative journalism; it was merely a matter of synthesizing information until a coherent narrative emerged. Something to consider when she quit her job at the hotel, if they didn't fire her first. She cleared her throat—raw and blistered after such a long night and so many more cigarettes than her habit usually demanded. "As a professional courtesy, we try to give everyone the opportunity to respond. Specifically, we're interested in why and how Project Honeydew continued recruiting human subjects after your IND was terminated by the FDA." It was Tamar who had followed the breadcrumbs to that particular bombshell. She'd sifted through Tom Kinnan's electronic dirty laundry, crawled around the Code of Federal Regulations Title 21, gone looking for Lockley's sticky fingerprints on any other clinical skulduggery documented in the CDER FOIA Electronic Reading Room. Lockley had been slapped on the wrist before for failing to comply with adverse event reporting requirements, which was probably why the FDA was quick to pull the plug on Honeydew. They didn't call it that in the official reports, of course—it seemed to be a pet name for the spur of her experiment that continued in secret and subterfuge. Kinnan had been copied on a string of testy emails between Lockley and the director of the Calhoun Center, who repeatedly refused to request a regulatory hearing to contest the termination of the trial. The discovery made Tamar dizzy with delight—curious whether the current director might be the same anonymous source who questioned Lockley's appointment in the *Belltower Times* two years ago. No wonder she'd tried to cover her tracks when everything went tits up. Or tails up, Tamar supposed.

Lockley's hands were shaking as she fumbled around for her keys again. "I'm sorry," she said, in a harsh little whisper, "but I really don't have time for this . . . nonsense."

"No comment, then?"

"Excuse me, I have a class to teach." Lockley wrenched the door open, and let it slam behind her. A few loose pages scuttled against the steps before the breeze wafted them across the quad, like so many letter-size tumbleweeds. Tamar fished her phone out of her pocket. *No comment*, she texted the rest of the Anchorites.

Edie was, of course, the first to respond. *All systems are go.*

Good, Tamar said. *I'm going to breakfast, if anyone wants to join me.*

She didn't expect anyone would but couldn't face returning to her empty apartment just yet. She wanted to celebrate, to congratulate herself on cracking the case and quitting her job and the first crisp, cold day of the rest of her life. She started walking back to Azalea Street, wondering what might satisfy her appetite.

When her phone buzzed again, it wasn't the Anchorites chat. Just Hannah, just her.

How about breakfast in bed?

7:00 AM
Tuck

Tuck jerked awake when something heavy landed on his stomach. He clawed the sleeping bag away from his face, trapped in darkness until he finally freed his head and his arms and realized his beanie had slipped down over his eyes. He pushed it up, shoved the alien mass off his lap. Thinking, unavoidably, of the rats, *the* rat, the rat who had crawled up his leg and into his hands and died there. The rat he would probably have nightmares about for the next two years, never mind the last few miserable hours.

That rat. He'd never had a rodent phobia before, but he was pretty sure he had one now.

Milky autumn sunlight dappled the floorboards through the colored glass. He rubbed his eyes until the room around him solidified, a thin veil of mist still blurring the world outside. The heavy thing in his lap was not a rat, he hoped. It was warm, oblong, slightly squishy, wrapped in tinfoil.

"Chill out, Churchmouse. It's a breakfast burrito, not a bomb."

Tuck squinted up at Theo, manspreading on the desk like anything less than a yard between his knees would be too close for comfort. Tuck shook his head. Still having a bad dream, maybe. "What are you doing in here?"

"Dude, what are *you* doing in here?"

"Sleeping," Tuck said. "Or I was. Finally. After being up all night with Edie."

Theo tossed a wad of napkins at him, held out a Styro-foam cup that smelled like coffee. Good coffee. Not instant. Tuck hated the way his mouth started to water immediately. He hadn't eaten anything but stale M&M's for dinner last night. He couldn't afford to refuse a free burrito, even if it came from Theo.

"Tamar tracked Lockley down," Theo told him, blow-ing on the second cup of coffee he'd brought for himself. "Declined to comment, of course."

"You couldn't have texted me that?" Tuck asked, grudgingly peeling foil off the top of the burrito. It warmed his fingers, and he simply held it in his swollen hands for a moment or two before tearing off a corner with his teeth.

"Been texting you for hours, bud," Theo said. "The whole group has."

"Phone's probably dead. Not a lot of outlets around here."

"Well, there are about to be a lot of outlets around here."

"What?" Tuck said, through bacon, egg, and what might have been mac and cheese. He could barely recognize the four food groups anymore. Or were there five? His last hot meal had been a hot dog from the 7-Eleven that tasted like it had been turning under the lamps for a month.

"News, Friar, news outlets. Edie's going to post her article posthaste. How long do you think it'll take for this place to be crawling with people? Not just media. Cops. Rubberneckers. Hazmat, maybe." He slurped his coffee. Raised his eyebrows.

"Okay, so I'll make myself scarce for a couple of days."

"And go where?" Theo folded his arms, pecs and biceps bulging under his sweatshirt. Still, the night had taken a toll on him, too. His perpetual five o'clock shadow was denser, darker, flecked with silver. Deep eyes dimmer, even the one that wasn't black tender and swollen, almost like he'd been crying.

"Dunno," Tuck said, and swallowed too much at once. "I'll figure something out." But it would be harder, more dangerous, as temperatures plummeted. Maybe it was time to pack his things and go south, like a migratory bird. But—as Theo had so gently inquired—to where? To what? He was an embarrassment to his family, and he'd rather be homeless than go crawling back to them anyway. Finding asylum at the Anchorite had conveniently deferred those dilemmas. Which was—he could at least admit to himself, if not to Theo—partly why he was so reluctant to leave. The world had no room for him, no use. It was easier to simply disappear.

"C'mon, you can't come back to this bolt-hole," Theo said. No grin for once, no trace of irony. "You can't live here forever."

Tuck stubbornly chewed, stubbornly swallowed. Closed up the tinfoil again, knowing he might need the rest of the burrito to stop his stomach snarling later. "I dunno," he said again, considering the problem of food if he decided to start hiking south. His mycological curiosity had started with foraging. He could live off the land with not much but his wits and his notebook for—well, a while, anyway. "I was doing just fine until you invited yourself in."

"Yeah, and who invited you?" Theo asked. "Saint Anthony?" He'd found Tuck's notebook on the desk and opened it without asking. Flipped through the first few pages, pausing on a colorful sketch of some turkey tail mushrooms, growing in their whimsical spirals.

"Your concern is touching," Tuck said, "but I'm fine. Really." He struggled to extract himself from the sleeping bag. Not thrilled to be standing there with his pale matchstick legs growing goose bumps in the chilly morning air while Theo was sitting there looking like a lump of grizzly bear. "I don't hate it here," he said, and tugged the note-book back. "I'm never bored."

"But you can go fuck around with moss or whatever it is you do anytime you feel like walking to a wooded area," Theo said, scowling now, like he was taking Tuck's stupidity personally. "You don't have to go native, dude."

"Then where do I go?" Tuck stowed his notebook on the bookshelf and reached for last night's jeans, still hang-ing over the back of the desk chair. Knees stained black with soil. He sighed. Clean clothes, like hot food and good coffee, were creature comforts long since given up for lost. "I appreciate the heads-up, but if I wanted help, I'd ask for it." He wasn't a charity case just yet. For all his failings, Tuck was resourceful. Mother Earth provided, if you knew where to look.

"Would you, though?" Theo said sourly. Unaccustomed to having his chivalrous advances so decisively rebuffed.

Tuck pretended to consider the question while he looked around the room, taking inventory of what he had to pack up or stash where nobody would be likely to find it in the likely event that someone like Edie, with more curiosity than sense, ignored the DANGER signs. "From you?" he said finally. "No." Wondering, once again, if out-right rudeness was the only way to discourage people who seemed so determined to meddle. Why couldn't they have sent Hannah? He'd found himself thinking wistfully of her cold-blooded apathy over the last seven hours.

"Fine," Theo said. "What if I'm asking *you* for help?"

Tuck almost laughed. Yeah, right. "With what?"

Theo shrugged, big shoulders bobbing up and back down again. "My best bartender just quit," he said. "Guess I never should have slept with her."

"She never should have slept with you."

"Yeah, she seemed to think so, too. Might try to change her mind, now th—" He realized he was thinking out loud. Tuck's turn to raise his eyebrows. "Never mind," Theo said. "Point is, I'm shorthanded and you're homeless. Maybe we can work out a"—he gestured toward the notebook—"what do you call it? A symbiotic arrangement."

Tuck was naturally suspicious, disinclined to believe him. But Theo's usual swagger and bluster had simmered down, tempered by stress or fatigue or—incredible as it seemed—a trace of genuine heartbreak. Tuck glanced out the window. The screech owls had gone silent, but the rest of the world was waking up. Half a mile east, the campus bell tower gave a few lugubrious *booms*. Seven o'clock. "Well, don't tell me how," he said, reaching for his coffee again with greater urgency. Wherever he went, he had no desire to be hanging around the Anchorite once the story broke.

"I know it's not your dream job, but you can pull a pint," Theo told him. "You can learn to mix a drink. Shit, I bet Noah would let you do the mushrooms if you really need some fungus to get fired up about."

"And live where? Last time I checked, not a lot of bartenders were making enough to make rent around here."

"I've got a spare room. It's not much, but it's better than this."

"You can't be serious."

"Like a heart attack, Tuck."

He couldn't remember the last time Theo had called him Tuck—not Friar, not Churchmouse, just Tuck. They stared at each other, disheveled and exhausted, each clutching their coffee in quiet desperation. It hadn't occurred to Tuck until just then that, despite his bustling bar, despite his animal magnetism, despite being such an obvious extrovert, maybe Theo kept coming back to the Anchorite because he was, in some bewildering way, *lonely*. Tuck cleared his throat.

"Did you make that burrito or pick it up somewhere?"

"Made it." Theo cleared his throat, too, avoiding Tuck's eyes, looking out the window at nothing. "Make burritos most mornings, with whatever's left over from last night."

"It's good," Tuck told him. "Thanks."

"Sure."

"Be better with mushrooms."

Theo looked back his way. "Maybe you can tell me if the ones growing behind my water heater are safe to eat."

"Hope so," Tuck told him. "Because I don't know anything about cocktails."

"Beggars can't be choosers," Theo said. "You're hired."

He slid off the desk, clapped Tuck on the shoulder so hard he thought he heard a floorboard crack beneath him. "Pack your shit, Churchmouse. You got a lot to learn by five o'clock."

Tuck checked his cheap watch. Consoled himself with a gulp of coffee and said, "Oh good, I regret this already."

Tamar's apartment had a lot of windows, which made it look bigger than it was. One bedroom, about five hundred square feet if Hannah had to guess, a corner unit on the second floor of an old mill building. Original hardwood, reddish in the late-morning sunlight. Exposed brick on two sides. Charming, if you didn't mind the mice in the walls or the cantankerous radiators or the pipe in the kitchen that was too hot to touch until it froze for the winter or hauling your laundry down four flights of stairs to a rank, frigid cellar, only to find that one of your two dozen neighbors had beaten you there. Old buildings were like that.

Hannah liked old buildings. Lots to listen to at night, a never-ending game of "What's that sound?" which gave her something to do in the rare dark hours she didn't spend driving around looking for lost souls with a penny for the ferryman. So to speak. She'd never been to Tamar's apartment during the day, wasn't sure why she'd suggested it, except for a reckless euphoria she'd brought back from Bothell Forest, as if she'd left her anger there with Kinnan. Hannah didn't take pride in much except making anybody dumb enough to fuck with her regret it. Preferably forever. No sign of her latest victim so far today, so far as she knew. Plenty left to worry about, but not now. Not yet.

She'd slept, but not long—surprised she was even able to doze off in an unfamiliar bed. Her own posed challenge enough but was at least equipped with all the usual—and unusual—interventions. Valley of the Dolls. You could drug yourself unconscious when nothing else worked, and by now nothing else did. She'd tried every humidifier and white noise machine and meditation app invented, and still the most reliable way to achieve oblivion was vodka and Klonopin and raspy AM radio in a language she didn't know. She couldn't get a prescription for anything anymore, but uppers and downers were there for the taking in any college town. One of the reasons she'd never mustered the willpower to pack up and leave.

When she woke, her eyes were glazed with dreams she didn't remember, the water-spotted ceiling coming slowly into focus. Unsure, at first, where she was. Startled to feel someone breathing beside her until she turned her head and saw Tamar's dark arm draped over a pillow in a graceful arc. Swimming through the linens. Hannah felt a little stupefied, by her and the sunlight. She had a soft spot for Tamar, mushy and tender as a bruise on an overripe peach. She hated liking people.

She rolled over, thumbed through the notifications on her phone. A few updates from the Anchorites. Edie alerting the media. Kinnan hadn't turned up and Tamar hadn't asked. This many hours later, Hannah could honestly say she didn't know where he was or care. She slid out from under the sheet and wandered into the living room.

Unsurprisingly, Tamar had books. Lots of books. Not nearly enough bookshelves. Even the kitchen counters were crowded with cookbooks and magazines. Who even got glossy magazines in the mail anymore? Hannah flicked through a copy of *Delayed Gratification*, with an article about Tolkien and artificial intelligence dog-eared in one corner. She glanced toward the bedroom. Surely Tamar had bookmarks. Perhaps it was gauche to use them in magazines. She thumbed through a few more pages, waiting for coffee to brew in an old-fashioned percolator. Everybody else had a Keurig or a Nespresso or some other complicated contraption with a name like an Alpine lap dog. Looking around in the daylight, she realized Tamar didn't have a TV. When would she watch it, between one desk jockey job and the other? But most people made time.

Hannah brewed her coffee so black and so strong it had stripped her stomach lining like turpentine. Surely a contributing factor to her ectomorphic vanishing act. Turn her sideways, and she disappears! Every few months she got another ulcer and spent a few weeks drinking broth and vomiting blood until it healed just enough for her to start smoking and guzzling coffee again. She rolled her eyes, flipped a page in the magazine. *But have you tried chamomile tea?*

She was, come to think of it, craving a cigarette. Probably time to make tracks. She didn't want to be there when Tamar woke up. Tamar didn't deserve that. Hannah wondered what the half-life of sleep was—how long it took before an hour of rest drained out of your body again. She'd only been up for thirty minutes and already the day was losing its luster. Sure, Kinnan might still be freezing his ass off somewhere in Bothell Forest, and the police might be digging up the Anchorite's backyard, and Heather might be scrambling to empty her desk before the mob with the torches and pitchforks arrived, but so what? That didn't change the prognosis. Hannah closed her eyes on the harsh, unwelcome sunshine. Rubbing her thumbs into her temples until they throbbed. Her memory of the night was mosaic, chimerical, distorted by that unparalleled intoxicant, retaliation. And what else? How could she know? Kinnan's strangled words echoed in her head. *Aggression. Hostility. Blindness.* Had he really said *cannibalism*, or was that just a figment of her demented fever dreams? She shoved the thought aside. That was a rat. That was different.

Hannah finished her coffee in three long swallows, left the magazine where she'd found it, and let herself into the bathroom. Wanting to wash her face, clear her head, rinse off the last ten hours. There was no counter space to speak of—only a shallow cabinet behind the mirror and whatever stowage could be had in the corners of the shower. She closed the door and pulled the cabinet open. Always interested to see what everybody else was taking, especially interested to see if there was anything worth taking with her when she left. Tamar, if she had any prescription medications, didn't keep them in the bathroom. Instead, she had a few makeup brushes and eye shadow palettes, though Hannah couldn't remember her ever wearing eye shadow, toothpaste and floss, a thermometer, and—aha—she knew she'd find something.

There was a small jewelry box on the bottom shelf. Not finished in velvet, but one of the white paper ones with a cotton liner on the bottom so what was inside didn't look so small, rolling around down there. Hannah popped the top off and was surprised again. Not pills or weed or even her old wedding ring, but a tiny blue eggshell, intact except for a hole in one end, like whatever was in there got one look at the world and decided not to come out. Oddly chastised by it—that delicate, innocent thing, boxed up like a secret—she put it back where she'd found it and closed the cabinet again.

She leaned back from her own reflection, which felt too close, too sudden. This morning's bedhead and last night's hat hair fighting for dominance. Her face always looked thin, drawn, sharp—her pointed nose and chin almost rat-like in their way, or so her sister always told her. Ratface.

Olive Oyl. Regan MacNeil. Her siblings picked the sweetest nicknames. But today her cheeks seemed softer. So did her mouth, her eyes, the slant of her brows. Everything a little bit . . . blurry.

Hannah turned the taps on and cupped cool water into her face, hoping it would wake her up. She liked Tamar, but she hated liking people, so she wanted to be gone. She shut the faucet off and lifted her head to look for a towel. But there was her reflection again, more clearly. Maybe. She leaned closer, close enough that her breath smudged the glass.

She froze there over the basin, water dripping from her chin. She tried to blink the blur away. Nothing happened. She raised one fingertip to the bridge of her nose and felt it—pale and scaly, but soft as warm candle wax.

Sleep in her eyes.

Acknowledgments

The writing of this book happened in strange fits and starts between June and December of 2023. It was a rough year for me, when writing was perpetually forced to compete with other big, life-altering things—selling my house, finishing my PhD, putting my whole life in storage, and spending a lot of time in hospitals for my dog's cancer treatment and my own recovery after shattering my left foot. Without the patience, support, and enthusiasm of my personal and professional networks I never would have survived the year, never mind writing two books at the same time. There were many long days and many sleepless nights; I was rarely at my best and often at my worst, and for some reason some people stuck with me anyway. This is as much their book as mine.

ACKNOWLEDGMENTS

Thanks first to my first reader, Arielle Datz, who has been my agent and the angel on my shoulder for ten whole years. I don't know how I got so lucky but I'm grateful every day to have her by my side. No less gratitude to my editor, Christine Kopprasch, and the whole team at Flatiron, who took a chance on this sight unseen, turned my restless ravings into something worth reading, and made it look so deliciously spooky inside and out. Away from the keyboard I, like the Anchorites, have my own insomniac support group to call on in the middle of the night: Adam and Adriana, Cary and Madison, James and Gram, the MedRen gang at UMD, and of course the Notorious cohort.

You are such stuff as dreams are made on.

Playlist

1. "Cruel Sun," Sparklehorse
2. "Waking Up," Elastica
3. "Cigarettes," X-Ray Spex
4. "She's a Hole," Oblivians
5. "Whistlin' Past the Graveyard," Tom Waits
6. "Thrill Kill," The Damned
7. "In the Night," Bauhaus
8. "Go Out," Blur
9. "Science Fiction," Arctic Monkeys
10. "Ghost Town," The Specials
11. "Pine Box Derby," Beat Happening
12. "Bury Me with It," Modest Mouse
13. "Dog New Tricks," Garbage
14. "There's a Moon On," Pixies

15. "Nightmare," The Rats
16. "Asleep at the Wheel," Band of Skulls
17. "Bloodletting (The Vampire Song)," Concrete Blonde
18. "Fell on Black Days," Soundgarden
19. "Revenge," Patti Smith
20. "Death to Our Friends," Sonic Youth
21. "Deadlines (Hostile)," Car Seat Headrest
22. "Doing It to Death," The Kills
23. "Wasted," Mazzy Star
24. "Little Beast," Elbow
25. "Dreams," Sebadoh
26. "Rest My Chemistry," Interpol
27. "Nocturnal Me," Echo & the Bunnymen
28. "Lullaby," The Cure
29. "Night Shift," Siouxsie and the Banshees
30. "Dream Baby Dream," Suicide

Cocktail Menu

Corpse Reviver #1

Serves 1

> 1½ ounce cognac
> ¾ ounce applejack
> ¾ ounce sweet vermouth
> Dash of orange bitters
> Orange peel, for garnish

Combine all ingredients in a mixing glass with ice and stir until chilled. Strain into a coupe glass and garnish with an orange peel.

For the Pavlopoulos Variation, triple the recipe and hold on to your liver.

Honeydew or Die

Serves 1

  1 ounce absinthe
  1 ounce white grape juice
  Squeeze of lime juice
  2 ounces ginger beer

Pour absinthe into a mixing glass over ice and stir until cloudy. Add white grape juice and lime juice and stir to combine. Strain into a champagne flute and top with ginger beer.

Read on for an excerpt of
M. L. Rio's *If We Were Villains*.

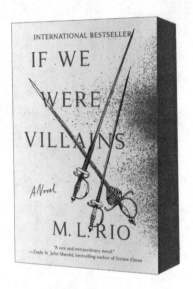

Copyright © 2017 by M. L. Rio

PROLOGUE

I sit with my wrists cuffed to the table and I think, *But that I am forbid / To tell the secrets of my prison-house, / I could a tale unfold whose lightest word / Would harrow up thy soul.* The guard stands by the door, watching me, like he's waiting for something to happen.

Enter Joseph Colborne. He is a graying man now, almost fifty. It's a surprise, every few weeks, to see how much he's aged—and he's aged a little more, every few weeks, for ten years. He sits across from me, folds his hands, and says, "Oliver."

"Joe."

"Heard the parole hearing went your way. Congratulations."

"I'd thank you if I thought you meant it."

"You know I don't think you belong in here."

"That doesn't mean you think I'm innocent."

"No." He sighs, checks his watch—the same one he's worn since we met—as if I'm boring him.

"So why are you here?" I ask. "Same fortnightly reason?"

His eyebrows make a flat black line. "You would say fucking 'fortnight.'"

"You can take the boy out of the theatre, or something like that."

He shakes his head, simultaneously amused and annoyed.

"Well?" I say.

"Well what?"

"*The gallows does well. But how does it well? It does well to those that do ill,*" I reply, determined to deserve his annoyance. "Why are you here? You should know by now I'm not going to tell you anything."

"Actually," he says, "this time I think I might be able to change your mind."

I sit up straighter in my chair. "How?"

"I'm leaving the force. Sold out, took a job in private security. Got my kids' education to think about."

For a moment I simply stare at him. Colborne, I always imagined, would have to be put down like a savage old dog before he'd leave the chief's office.

"How's that supposed to persuade me?" I ask.

"Anything you say will be strictly off the record."

"Then why bother?"

He sighs again and all the lines on his face deepen. "Oliver, I don't care about doling out punishment, not anymore. Someone served the time, and we rarely get that much satisfaction in our line of work. But I don't want to hang up my hat and waste the next ten years wondering what really happened ten years ago."

I say nothing at first. I like the idea but don't trust it. I glance around at the grim cinder blocks, the tiny black video cameras that peer down from every corner, the guard with his jutting underbite. I close my eyes, inhale deeply, and imagine the freshness of Illinois springtime, what it will be like to step outside after gasping on stale prison air for a third of my life.

When I exhale I open my eyes and Colborne is watching me closely.

"I don't know," I say. "I'm getting out of here, one way or the other. I don't want to risk coming back. Seems safer to let sleeping dogs lie."

His fingers drum restlessly on the table. "Tell me something," he says. "Do you ever lie in your cell, staring up at the ceiling, wondering how you wound up in here, and you can't sleep because you can't stop thinking about that day?"

"Every night," I say, without sarcasm. "But here's the difference, Joe. For you it was just one day, then business as usual. For us it was one day, and every single day that came after." I lean forward on my elbows, so my face is only a few inches from his, so he hears every word when I lower my voice. "It must eat you alive, not knowing. Not knowing who, not knowing how, not knowing why. But you didn't know *him*."

He wears a strange, queasy expression now, as if I've become unspeakably ugly and awful to look at. "You've kept your secrets all this time," he says. "It would drive anyone else crazy. Why do it?"

"I wanted to."

"Do you still?"

My heart feels heavy in my chest. Secrets carry weight, like lead.

I lean back. The guard watches impassively, as if we're two strangers talking in another language, our conversation distant and insignificant. I think of the others. Once upon a time, *us*. We did wicked things, but they were necessary, too—or so it seemed. Looking back, years later, I'm not so sure they were, and now I wonder: Could I explain it all to Colborne, the little twists and turns and final *exodos*? I study his blank open face, the gray eyes winged now by crow's-feet, but clear and bright as they have always been.

"All right," I say. "I'll tell you a story. But you have to understand a few things."

Colborne is motionless. "I'm listening."

"First, I'll start talking after I get out of here, not before. Second, this can't come back to me or anyone else—no double jeopardy. And last, it's not an apology."

I wait for some response from him, a nod or a word, but he only blinks at me, silent and stoic as a sphinx.

"Well, Joe?" I say. "Can you live with that?"

He gives me a cold sliver of a smile. "Yes, I think I can."

SCENE 1

The time: September 1997, my fourth and final year at Dellecher Classical Conservatory. The place: Broadwater, Illinois, a small town of almost no consequence. It had been a warm autumn so far.

Enter the players. There were seven of us then, seven bright young things with wide precious futures ahead of us, though we saw no farther than the books in front of our faces. We were always surrounded by books and words and poetry, all the fierce passions of the world bound in leather and vellum. (I blame this in part for what happened.) The Castle library was an airy octagonal room, walled with bookshelves, crowded with sumptuous old furniture, and kept drowsily warm by a monumental fireplace that burned almost constantly, regardless of the temperature outside. The clock on the mantel struck twelve, and we stirred, one by one, like seven statues coming to life.

"*'Tis now dead midnight*," Richard said. He sat in the largest armchair like it was a throne, long legs outstretched, feet propped up on the grate. Three years of playing kings and conquerors had taught him to sit that way in every chair, onstage or off. "And by eight o'clock tomorrow we must be made immortal." He closed his book with a snap.

Meredith, curled like a cat on one end of the sofa (while I sprawled like a dog on the other), toyed with one strand of her long auburn hair as she asked, "Where are you going?"

Richard: "*Weary with toil, I haste me to my bed—*"

Filippa: "Spare us."

Richard: "Early morning and all that."

Alexander: "He says, as if he's concerned."

Wren, sitting cross-legged on a cushion by the hearth and

oblivious to the others' bickering, said, "Have you all picked your pieces? I can't decide."

Me: "What about Isabella? Your Isabella's excellent."

Meredith: "*Measure*'s a comedy, you fool. We're auditioning for *Caesar*."

"I don't know why we bother auditioning at all." Alexander—slumped over the table, wallowing in the darkness at the back of the room—reached for the bottle of Scotch at his elbow. He refilled his glass, took one huge gulp, and grimaced at the rest of us. "I could cast the whole bastarding thing right now."

"How?" I asked. "I never know where I'll end up."

"That's because they always cast you last," Richard said, "as whatever happens to be left over."

"Tsk-tsk," Meredith said. "Are we Richard tonight or are we Dick?"

"Ignore him, Oliver," James said. He sat by himself in the farthest corner, loath to look up from his notebook. He had always been the most serious student in our year, which (probably) explained why he was also the best actor and (certainly) why no one resented him for it.

"There." Alexander had unfolded a wad of ten-dollar bills from his pocket and was counting them out on the table. "That's fifty dollars."

"For what?" Meredith said. "You want a lap dance?"

"Why, are you practicing for after graduation?"

"Bite me."

"Ask nicely."

"Fifty dollars for what?" I said, keen to interrupt. Meredith and Alexander had by far the foulest mouths among the seven of us, and took a perverse kind of pride in out-cussing each other. If we let them, they'd go at it all night.

Alexander tapped the stack of tens with one long finger. "I bet fifty dollars I can call the cast list right now and not be wrong."

Five of us exchanged curious glances; Wren was still frowning into the fireplace.

"All right, let's hear it," Filippa said, with a wan little sigh, as though her curiosity had gotten the better of her.

Alexander pushed his unruly black curls back from his face and said, "Well, obviously Richard will be Caesar."

"Because we all secretly want to kill him?" James asked.

Richard arched one dark eyebrow. "*Et tu, Bruté?*"

"*Sic semper tyrannis,*" James said, and drew the tip of his pen across his throat like a dagger. *Thus always to tyrants.*

Alexander gestured from one of them to the other. "Exactly," he said. "James will be Brutus because he's always the good guy, and I'll be Cassius because I'm always the bad guy. Richard and Wren can't be married because that would be gross, so she'll be Portia, Meredith will be Calpurnia, and Pip, you'll end up in drag again."

Filippa, more difficult to cast than Meredith (the femme fatale) or Wren (the ingénue), was obliged to cross-dress whenever we ran out of good female parts—a common occurrence in the Shakespearean theatre. "Kill me," she said.

"Wait," I said, effectively proving Richard's hypothesis that I was a permanent leftover in the casting process, "where does that leave me?"

Alexander studied me with narrowed eyes, running his tongue across his teeth. "Probably as Octavius," he decided. "They won't make you Antony—no offense, but you're just not *conspicuous* enough. It'll be that insufferable third-year, what's his name?"

Filippa: "Richard the Second?"

Richard: "Hilarious. No, Colin Hyland."

"Spectacular." I looked down at the text of *Pericles* I was scanning, for what felt like the hundredth time. Only half as talented as any of the rest of them, I seemed doomed to always play supporting roles in someone else's story. Far too many times I had asked myself whether art was imitating life or if it was the other way around.

Alexander: "Fifty bucks, on that exact casting. Any takers?"

Meredith: "No."

Alexander: "Why not?"

Filippa: "Because that's precisely what'll happen."

Richard chuckled and climbed out of his chair. "One can only hope." He started toward the door and leaned over to pinch James's cheek on his way out. "*Goodnight, sweet prince*—"

James smacked Richard's hand away with his notebook, then made a show of disappearing behind it again. Meredith echoed Richard's laugh and said, "*Thou art as hot a Jack in thy mood as any in Italy!*"

"*A plague o' both your houses,*" James muttered.

Meredith stretched—with a small, suggestive groan—and pushed herself off the couch.

"Coming to bed?" Richard asked.

"Yes. Alexander's made all this work seem rather pointless." She left her books scattered on the low table in front of the fire, her empty wineglass with them, a crescent of lipstick clinging to the rim. "Goodnight," she said, to the room at large. "Godspeed." They disappeared down the hall together.

I rubbed my eyes, which were beginning to burn from the effort of reading for hours on end. Wren tossed her book backward over her head, and I started as it landed beside me on the couch.

Wren: "To hell with it."

Alexander: "That's the spirit."

Wren: "I'll just do Isabella."

Filippa: "Just go to bed."

Wren stood slowly, blinking the vestigial light of the fire out of her eyes. "I'll probably lie awake all night reciting lines," she said.

"Want to come out for a smoke?" Alexander had finished his

whiskey (again) and was rolling a spliff on the table. "Might help you relax."

"No, thank you," she said, drifting out into the hall. "Good-night."

"Suit yourself." Alexander pushed his chair back, spliff poking out of one corner of his mouth. "Oliver?"

"If I help you smoke that I'll wake up with no voice tomorrow."

"Pip?"

She nudged her glasses up into her hair and coughed softly, testing her throat. "God, you're a terrible influence," she said. "Fine."

He nodded, already halfway out of the room, hands buried deep in his pockets. I watched them go, a little jealously, then slumped down against the arm of the couch. I struggled to focus on my text, which was so aggressively annotated that it was barely legible anymore.

PERICLES: *Antioch, farewell! for wisdom sees those men*
Blush not in actions blacker than the night
Will 'schew no course to keep them from the light.
One sin, I know, another doth provoke;
Murder's as near to lust as flame to smoke.

I murmured the last two lines under my breath. I knew them by heart, had known them for months, but the fear that I would forget a word or phrase halfway through my audition gnawed at me anyway. I glanced across the room at James and said, "Do you ever wonder if Shakespeare knew these speeches half as well as we do?"

He withdrew from whatever verse he was reading, looked up, and said, "Constantly."

I cracked a smile, vindicated just enough. "Well, I give up. I'm not actually getting anything done."

He checked his watch. "No, I don't think I am either."

I heaved myself off the sofa and followed James up the spiral stairs to the bedroom we shared—which was directly over the library, the highest of three rooms in a little stone column commonly referred to as the Tower. It had once been used only as an attic, but the cobwebs and clutter had been cleared away to make room for more students in the late seventies. Twenty years later it housed James and me, two beds with blue Dellecher bedspreads, two monstrous old wardrobes, and a pair of mismatched bookshelves too ugly for the library.

"Do you think it'll fall out how Alexander says?" I asked.

James pulled his shirt off, mussing his hair in the process. "If you ask me, it's too predictable."

"When have they ever surprised us?"

"Frederick surprises me all the time," he said. "But Gwendolyn will have the final say, she always does."

"If it were up to her, Richard would play all of the men and half the women."

"Which would leave Meredith playing the other half." He pressed the heels of his palms against his eyes. "When do you read tomorrow?"

"Right after Richard. Filippa's after me."

"And I'm after her. God, I feel bad for her."

"Yeah," I said. "It's a wonder she hasn't dropped out."

James frowned thoughtfully as he wriggled out of his jeans. "Well, she's a bit more resilient than the rest of us. Maybe that's why Gwendolyn torments her."

"Just because she can take it?" I said, discarding my own clothes in a pile on the floor. "That's cruel."

He shrugged. "That's Gwendolyn."

"If I had my way, I'd turn it all upside down," I said. "Make Alexander Caesar and have Richard play Cassius instead."

He folded his comforter back and asked, "Am I still Brutus?"

"No." I tossed a sock at him. "You're Antony. For once I get to be the lead."

"Your time will come to be the tragic hero. Just wait for spring."

I glanced up from the drawer I was pawing through. "Has Frederick been telling you secrets again?"

He lay down and folded his hands behind his head. "He may have mentioned *Troilus and Cressida*. He has this fantastic idea to do it as a battle of the sexes. All the Trojans men, all the Greeks women."

"That's insane."

"Why? That play is as much about sex as it is about war," he said. "Gwendolyn will want Richard to be Hector, of course, but that makes you Troilus."

"Why on earth wouldn't *you* be Troilus?"

He shifted, arched his back. "I may have mentioned that I'd like to have a little more variety on my résumé."

I stared at him, unsure if I should be insulted.

"Don't look at me like that," he said, a low note of reproach in his voice. "He agreed we all need to break out of our boxes. I'm tired of playing fools in love like Troilus, and I'm sure you're tired of always playing the sidekick."

I flopped on my bed on my back. "Yeah, you're probably right." For a moment I let my thoughts wander, and then I breathed out a laugh.

"Something funny?" James asked, as he reached over to turn out the light.

"You'll have to be Cressida," I told him. "You're the only one of us pretty enough."

We lay there laughing in the dark until we dropped off to sleep, and slept deeply, with no way of knowing that the curtain was about to rise on a drama of our own invention.

About the Author

M. L. Rio holds an MA in Shakespeare studies from King's College London and Shakespeare's Globe and a PhD in English from the University of Maryland, College Park. Her bestselling first novel, *If We Were Villains*, has been published in twenty countries and eighteen languages. *Graveyard Shift* is her first novella.